What the critics are saying…

"A well-written story, it is both exciting and suspenseful." ~ *Romance Review Today*

Gold Star Award "Ms. O'Clare has really outdone herself with this book. I have enjoyed all of her work that I have been able to read thus far, but this is the best one yet." ~ *Just Erotic Romance Reviews*

Five Coffee Cup "Ms O'Clare has written a sensual and extraordinary story of how love can creep up on the most unsuspecting person." ~ *Coffee Time Romance*

Lorie O'Clare

Fallen Gods II

Jaded Prey

An Ellora's Cave Romantica Publication

www.ellorascave.com

Fallen Gods: Jaded Prey

ISBN # 1419952145

Edited by: Sue-Ellen Gower
Cover art by: Syneca

Electronic book Publication: November, 2004
Trade paperback Publication: June, 2005

Warning:

The following material contains graphic sexual content meant for mature readers. *Jaded Prey* has been rated *E-rotic* by a minimum of three independent reviewers.

Ellora's Cave Publishing offers three levels of Romantica™ reading entertainment: S (S-ensuous), E (E-rotic), and X (X-treme).

S-e*nsuous* love scenes are explicit and leave nothing to the imagination.

E-*rotic* love scenes are explicit, leave nothing to the imagination, and are high in volume per the overall word count. In addition, some E-rated titles might contain fantasy material that some readers find objectionable, such as bondage, submission, same sex encounters, forced seductions, etc. E-rated titles are the most graphic titles we carry; it is common, for instance, for an author to use words such as "fucking", "cock", "pussy", etc., within their work of literature.

X-*treme* titles differ from E-rated titles only in plot premise and storyline execution. Unlike E-rated titles, stories designated with the letter X tend to contain controversial subject matter not for the faint of heart.

Also by Lorie O'Clare:

Fallen Gods: Tainted Purity

Fallen Gods: Lotus Blooming

Lunewulf 1: Pack Law

Lunewulf 2: In Her Blood

Lunewulf 3: In Her Dreams

Lunewulf 4: In Her Nature

Lunewulf 5: In Her Soul

Full Moon Rising

Things That Go Bump in the Night 2004 anthology

Sex Slaves 1: Sex Traders

Sex Slaves 2: Waiting For Yesterday

Sex Slaves 3: Waiting for Dawn

Torrid Love: The First Time

Torrid Love: Caught!

Jaded Prey

Fallen Gods

Trademarks Acknowledgement

The author acknowledges the trademarked status and trademark owners of the following wordmarks mentioned in this work of fiction:

Jeep: Daimler Chrysler Corporation

Corvette: General Motors Corporation

Chapter One

Incense burnt thick through the air, its aroma wrapping around Naomi, pulling her in like a guiding spirit. The two small lamps offered little light. Everyone else in the room seemed oblivious to her, swaying and moaning, their eyes closed, talking to the gods who had been called forth.

Glancing at the high priestess, Naomi Lorghon wondered again why she had agreed to come to this ceremony.

"Inanna, we call you forth." Oblivious to the rest of them, the high priestess stood in the middle of the circle, her arms extended. "Grace us with your presence while we honor you, repeating your ceremony, making our covens stronger by uniting as you did."

Naomi closed her eyes, knowing she should feel something when everyone around her grew silent, their breathing increasing. Her heart raced, fear suddenly gripping her. They would know she wasn't part of them—that she shouldn't really be there.

"I am ready for you." The high priestess also spoke through heavy pants. The floorboards creaked, indicating she had climbed onto the small cot set up in the middle of the circle. "Moisture seeps from me, preparing me. My skin is moist from my cream. My sensitive muscles swell, the craving to unite consuming me. Who will enter and claim what I offer?"

Naomi dared open one eye, peeking at the lady who adjusted herself on the cot, her naked body shadowed by the dim lighting in the room. But when she did, Naomi couldn't look away. The high priestess, the leader of the coven her friend had invited her to join, relaxed on the cot, staring upward at the ceiling while she held out her hands. Her small breasts were firm, her nipples erect, while she panted, parting her legs, allowing everyone to see the damp hair covering her mound.

The woman's body arched, her breathing visible as her chest expanded, the outline of her breasts shadowed by the dim lighting. Naomi found herself matching the woman's breath, watching her, studying her naked body. She couldn't help comparing notes on how she knew she looked naked.

Naomi liked to keep herself shaved, but found herself entranced, staring at the woman while her insides grew warm. Maybe she was being affected by the magic floating through the room. Or maybe she was simply aroused, knowing what was about to happen.

"I will claim what you have to offer. Entering you, our covens will grow in strength." A man stepped forward, unbuttoning his pants while moving to stand over the high priestess. "Have you properly prepared the bed for me?"

"I have," she answered, turning her attention to him. "Anointed and blessed, I lay on the bed where you will have me."

Naomi fisted her hands on either side of her, her palms growing damp, making her itch to rub her hands together but daring not to move. She swallowed, her mouth suddenly dry while she stared at the man's cock, which appeared like an eager shaft when he let his pants fall to his ankles.

"Herne the Hunter breathes through me, anxious to enter you, to strengthen our union." The man stepped out of his pants and crawled over the woman.

The group around them began moaning again, a few around her swaying while Naomi forgot about being discreet with her watching.

"Inanna comes forth, blessing this union, making us stronger." The high priestess reached for the man, pulling him to her.

Naomi had never watched two people fuck before. And although her friend Thena had told her what would happen before they arrived, Naomi still had a hard time believing that she was witnessing this.

She'd always considered herself almost a prude. Sure, sex excited her. But it took so much work to find a boyfriend, and then most of them turned out to be creeps. She couldn't remember the last time she'd had sex.

But here, watching these two, this high priest and high priestess, uniting to strengthen their covens, and bring unity to all who were members, her insides spilled over with an awakening she hadn't expected.

Thena began moaning quietly next to Naomi. She glanced her way, watching her friend rub her hands over her breasts, bringing her nipples to hard peaks through her shirt. But Thena didn't look at her. All of her attention was on the couple in the middle of the circle.

Naomi looked back at them, watching with heated amazement while they caressed each other, loving each other openly and without hesitation.

"We must unite now," the high priest uttered, his name escaping Naomi at the moment. He ran his hands along the high priestess's inner thighs. "With the presence of Herne the Hunter—"

"—and the goddess, Inanna," the high priestess said on a gasp.

"We unite our covens, bringing us strength with the grace of the gods." The high priest looked up to the ceiling at the same time he drove deep inside the high priestess's pussy.

Everyone in the room gasped. Naomi right along with them. For she swore she felt her own pussy swell, her moisture soaking her silk undies while a pressure grew inside her.

The room suddenly was too warm, while her heart raced watching the couple fuck on the cot in front of her. She glanced around the room, wanting to give them privacy but at the same time knowing they wanted to be watched.

Blood rushed through her. Her heart pumped faster, while her breath came in heavy sighs. She wouldn't play with herself. There was no way she would squeeze her suddenly swollen breasts. And no matter how much her pussy ached, her cream soaking her shaven skin making her undies cling to her, she wouldn't slide her fingers under her clothing and stroke the need that blossomed with a fury that made her want to cry out.

Watching the couple move together, the high priestess's legs spread open, her feet arched while the man pounded her hard and with a steady rhythm, made Naomi ache for a cock to be buried deep inside her.

She fought for her breath, closing her eyes while imagining a man touching her the way the high priest fondled the high priestess on the cot. Strong firm hands caressing her, burning her skin with his touch. Fingers gracing over her, feverishly, drawing a craving from deep within her.

"Oh, yes. Yes!" The high priestess called out, her voice clear and strong, bringing everyone in the room to attention.

Gasps were held. Swaying stopped. All watched her climax, her body arching underneath her lover.

"You like that, don't you?" the high priest growled, burying his cock deep inside her.

Naomi put her hand over her mouth, swearing she was spread open deep inside, feeling a large cock buried deep inside her. It was all she could do to keep standing, to not stumble, fall over from the intensity of a large cock brushing against the sensitive walls inside her.

The high priestess cried out, coming while everyone watched. At the same moment, everything inside Naomi seemed to explode. A whimper escaped her, heat flushing through her that she couldn't keep her emotions at bay while the couple in front of her climaxed together.

Her friend Thena let out a sigh, glancing at her with a small smile before returning her attention to the couple.

"And so it is." The high priest moved to his knees, pulling the high priestess up with him, cradling her while he looked at everyone around them with a sated grin. "We unite our covens, growing in strength, praising the gods and goddesses for blessing us with their strength."

"Blessed be," several around Naomi murmured.

The high priest pulled the high priestess to her feet. Joining the others in the circle, Naomi took Thena's hand, aware of how warm her touch was. She didn't know the person on her other side, but felt their heat as well. The warmth that traveled through her, searing through her skin as if she were on fire, made her feel dizzy.

She barely heard the blessing, the joyous praise of the covens united, or the thanking of the gods for giving them the gifts of their strength.

"Are you okay?" Thena asked her, brushing her fingers down Naomi's face while moving strands of hair that had loosened from her braids out of the way.

"Yes. I'm fine." Although she was anything but fine.

What the hell just happened? She'd never been to a witch's coven before. Her friend Thena never hid her involvement or her faith. She was a good person, and Naomi had never judged her for her practicing witchcraft. But never once, not in a million years, had she imagined a coven could make her feel like this. It was as if she had been the one on the cot, as if she had just been thoroughly fucked.

"There's food in the other room." Thena nudged her, smiling the way she always did as if they were on their way to the break room at work.

Naomi followed her friend into the family room. She didn't know the people who lived here, or for that matter most of the people who had been part of the coven. But the chatter was amiable, a lively discussion of city politics quickly picking up, and how they would have to do a blessing on their candidate of choice.

The couple on the cot had disappeared, more than likely to shower, or continue their lovemaking in a more private setting. Naomi accepted her plate, moving around the table with the others and helping herself to small portions of the varieties of foods offered.

But she wasn't hungry, at least not for food. Maybe she'd gone too long without sex. Maybe her hunger had been dormant, and having been awakened, now she couldn't be still. Restless and feeling on edge, she worked her way through the group and decided fresh air was in order. Anything to calm the pounding of her heart. Her blood pressure would soar through the ceiling at this rate.

Naomi slid out on to the back patio, the few people who were outside having escaped for a cigarette. Well, it was nice to know they at least had gained enough satisfaction to enjoy a smoke after their sexual voyeurism.

Cold evening air made her eyes water instantly. Nothing would soothe the fire burning through her, though. Why the hell had she agreed to come here?

"Enjoying yourself?" someone asked from behind her.

Naomi turned, and then looked up at the tall, well-built man standing behind her. Her mouth went dry and her fingers started to tremble. Looking down quickly, she gripped her plate so as not to make a fool of herself by spilling food at the man's feet.

And that would be just like her. The best-looking man she'd ever laid eyes on just said something to her, and she almost embarrassed herself.

"Excuse me?" she croaked, and then cleared her throat, feeling a flush of heat rush over her cheeks.

The man smiled, taking her plate from her before she realized what he'd done. His fingers brushed over hers, torturing her with a heat that swept through her making her suddenly way too warm. It was time to get out of there. Nothing good could happen when she was so flustered.

"I asked if you were enjoying yourself?" he spoke again, his words a soft caress teasing her overstimulated senses.

"Sure. Thanks for asking." She tried to swallow the lump in her throat while staring into his dark brooding expression.

"Just watching isn't for everyone." He lowered his voice, whispering so only she could hear.

Naomi swallowed again, his green eyes searching her face while the slightest of smiles made his mouth curve—an absolutely beautiful mouth, lips full but not too full. He was probably a damned good kisser.

"But that's what we were invited to do." Talking about this made her nervous.

Or maybe it was the way he looked at her, a predator waiting to devour his prey. Thick dark hair bordered his face, a well-chiseled face with smooth, dark olive skin. She needed to look away from him. It was rude to stare. But never had she stared at such pure perfection.

"And what if I invited you to do more?" His whisper tortured her, his deep baritone a husky sound that grated over her, ravishing her with its sound.

She followed the movement of his hand, lowering her gaze when he reached down, taking her long braid in his hand, brushing against the swell of her breast with his touch.

Naomi took a step backwards, frustration doing nothing to soothe the ache that seemed to be ready to explode inside her. It wasn't fair that even the gorgeous ones had to be jerks.

"No, thank you," she mumbled, leaving her plate behind while she hurried back into the house.

There was no way she could eat a bite of anything now.

Chapter Two

Merco watched the sexy little redhead march away from him. She struggled with the sliding door for a moment, her irritation growing. He almost moved to help her but decided to let her take her frustration out on the door, instead of berating him for his forwardness.

Disappearing, he reappeared in the living room, taking in the nice view of her ass while she said some hurried words to one of her friends. No one else in the room noticed him. Not that he was too surprised by that. The amount of magic actually existing among these people would fit in his little finger.

But the sexy redhead, not even a member of either coven, saw him. Her pure, untouched energy would be swallowed up whole by this group of hopefuls. Just by watching them, enjoying how they reenacted the ancient ritual of uniting powers, most everyone in the room wished and prayed for powers they would never possess or understand.

Not the redhead. She didn't even want to be there. The way the ceremony moved her hadn't surprised him. And even now, while she worked so hard to sound calm, her insides burned with a need she wouldn't be able to satisfy. No toy could take away the hunger eating at her.

"Thanks for inviting me, Thena," she said to a pretty black lady who licked chocolate from her fingers. "But I'm tired. Working days now is taking its toll on me."

"Yeah, and we miss you on third shift, too." The woman had a sultry chuckle, confident and relaxed. "But I'm glad you came tonight. No pun intended."

This time the redhead laughed with her, letting her guard down slightly. He moved closer, focusing on the smooth curve of her ass. She looked damned good in her jeans, with her sweater clinging to her, showing off how slim and fit she was. He'd love to see how she looked with that long thick hair let loose, and not bound in braids the way she had it now. Just imagining those thick locks streaming over her creamy white skin made his cock hard.

Her laugh vibrated through him, catching him off-guard. Merco ignored the others lingering around him, chatting about trivial things. They didn't see him anyway.

"Thanks for inviting me." Her voice was so soft, uncertainty lingering around her.

Her fingers moved through the loose strands around her face, stroking them into place. They trembled slightly, and she shoved her hands into her jean pockets quickly.

"Next month, we'll have a regular meeting. It would be great if you came back." Thena walked with her toward the door, the two women contrasting each other nicely with their dark and fair features.

Merco followed, moving outside with the two of them. Both women wrapped their arms around themselves, fighting off the night chill.

"Okay. Well, I'll talk to you soon." She waved and hurried toward the street to a small car.

She almost dropped her keys when she noticed him. Even in the dark, her blue eyes were beautiful, so large, surrounded by such creamy white skin and thick long hair that shone like dark rubies under the streetlights. Everything about her captivated him.

Maybe it had been too long since he'd been with a human. There was a sense of defiance about her. If he reached too deeply into her thoughts, he feared he might hurt her, overwhelm her with his power, yet she glared at him as if she could take him down with one solid punch. And the thought had crossed her mind.

"You're following me," she accused unnecessarily. "What is it about 'no' that you don't understand?"

"Your mind and body say yes, so why should I pay attention to your words?" He was amused. That was it. Usually women begged him to fuck them. This little spitfire was a nice change of pace.

"You're wrong. Leave me alone." She fumbled with her keys for a moment until she managed to unlock her car then she got in and reached to pull the door closed.

Merco grabbed her car door, staring down at her long thin legs when she pulled them into the car. He squatted down, those ravenous blue eyes, and pouty full lips captivating him. She didn't wear any makeup, and her hair hardly did her justice in the tomboy-style braids, but her incredible beauty stood out regardless of how little she worked to display herself.

"I haven't been wrong in a very long time." He almost said centuries until he realized she was frightened.

Her sexual energy swam around her in such a thick haze that it was impossible to miss. But he'd scared her, and for whatever reasons wanted to reassure her all he offered was satisfaction to her burning needs.

"You need a good fucking. Your body is screaming for it. All I'm offering to do is help you." He smiled, sending thoughts to calm her down.

She turned quickly, raising her hand and balling it into a fist. When she aimed to hit him, his shock almost got him a bloody nose. Now wouldn't that just make him the laughing stock of the Ancients?

He grabbed her hand, careful not to crush her fragile bones. Her soft skin caressed his senses. Running his thumb over the smoothness of her skin, fire burned through him, a need ravaging his libido unlike anything he'd experienced. And he'd had a lot of experiences.

She yanked her hand back, but he tightened his grip, unwilling to let her go.

"If you don't let go, I swear I'll scream," she hissed through her teeth.

The way her breathing increased, as lust pumped through her body, made her chest rise and fall in a rapid flutter, her breasts stretching the material of her shirt to its limit. He itched to make her clothing disappear, to see her in her full beauty.

"I have no doubts you will scream. You haven't experienced true pleasure for quite a while. That tight pussy of yours is itching to explode." He held her hand, feeling her skin warm further under his touch.

Her thoughts were so fogged with lust, he wasn't prepared for her leg to come out of the car. She moved quickly, her blue eyes burning with a fiery passion. In the next second she kicked him, hard, and square on the knee.

"If you think lines like this will get you a piece of ass, your brain must be smaller than your cock." She slammed the door on him, and started her car with a fury.

In the next second she squealed off, leaving him in a cloud of exhaust.

Merco straightened, the dull throb in his knee not bothering him as much as her flat-out rejection for him to soothe her cravings. What was it about the women on this planet? They wanted to be fucked more than anything. Her thoughts were an open book. Yet she repeatedly denied to him that she wanted him. She lied.

Staring back at the house, he knew nothing inside had impressed him. He'd enjoyed the reenactment of the sexual uniting of the covens, but none of the women had called him forth like the fiery redhead.

Other orgies were going on in this town. Kansas City seemed to have its share of them. Merco faded into the breeze, allowing the human form he had taken to vanish. For some reason, he couldn't get his thoughts of the redhead to vanish as easily though. Something about her had gotten to him. And it might just amuse him to explore it a bit further.

He knew he would go after her. It just never occurred to him that she would go straight to the building some of the other Ancients had under protection. His friends Braze and Bridget were in one of the apartments here. Maybe they would offer some entertainment—distract him from the human who had run from him.

Merco chuckled. He couldn't even bring himself to accept the fact that she'd straight-out rejected his ass—then she'd run from him.

Pushing his way through the protective barrier that encompassed the apartment building would alert his fellow coven members of his presence. That didn't bother him. Merco looked at it as a type of doorbell, announcing his presence.

Putting a smile on his face, he materialized into the living room of the small apartment where the two of them seemed content to live. His entire mood lifted at the sight of Bridget on her knees, sucking Braze's cock.

"I've arrived just in time." He relaxed onto their couch, kicking his legs up and situating himself.

This was just what he needed, relaxed downtime with his friends. His cock danced to life at the sight of his friend's lover and life partner. The two of them made an incredible couple, loving each other with the aggressiveness seldom found in two people who had been together for so long.

Bridget coughed and gagged, Braze's hard cock pressed deep into her mouth. The two of them acknowledged him with quick glances. Bridget waved her hand at him and suddenly he could no longer see.

"Hey!" he yelled, reaching up to yank at the blindfold securely tied around his head. "That's not fair."

By the time he'd yanked it off, both of them were dressed.

"Tell me about it," Braze grumbled, looking down at the clothes on his body. His irritation showed when he turned his attention to Merco. "This better be good."

"I got rejected." There—he'd said it. He'd admitted it out loud.

Bridget stared at him for a moment, her hands slowly moving to the soft curve of her hips.

"Let me get this right," she began.

"I know…I know." He wished he could get the event of meeting the redhead out of his thoughts. He kept replaying their moments together over in his head. "I can't believe it, either."

"Why you little pompous ass." Bridget threw her hands up in the air, her expression darkening. "You interrupted us to whine about some woman telling you no?"

Merco stared at her. Actually yes, he had. But he wasn't whining, was he?

This wasn't the reaction he'd expected. An uncomfortable warmth traveled through him while he looked from one of them to the other. Braze's emotions were at bay, his expression serious. Merco waved his hand so that several drinks appeared. Bridget looked at him in disgust and waved the drinks away.

"Merco. You have become a spoiled-rotten child. I can only imagine what you might have done to get yourself rejected." She looked angry now, angry enough to throw him out. And he knew she had a better punch than that redhead did.

"I simply offered to take care of her needs." Merco shrugged, although a thought slowly crept into his mind that maybe he'd been a bit pushy. "I've never had problems before," he added quickly, suddenly feeling the need to defend his actions.

Braze coughed, but didn't say anything. He didn't have to. Bridget's look of contempt spoke loud enough for both of them.

"You just walked up to a human and said, 'come here, baby, and I'll fuck you'?" She made it sound rather repulsive.

"Okay. Maybe I came on a bit strong." He offered her his winning smile.

"I'm surprised she didn't slap you in the face." Bridget turned from him, pacing toward the kitchen door, her long hair swaying down her back.

Merco thought again how the redhead would look with her hair free to flow.

"What were you thinking?" Bridget adjusted a picture hanging on the wall and then faced him. "You didn't do anything… I mean…you didn't…"

"No. I didn't force her. You know rape isn't my style." And he wouldn't tell her he'd intercepted the slap. "She kicked me in the knee," he said, somehow knowing that wouldn't get him any sympathy.

Braze broke out laughing and Bridget glared at him.

"It sounds to me like you deserved it. You can't treat human women that way, Merco. They are independent. Just because you can feel their lust doesn't mean they are going to spread their legs for you."

"It's true of all women… All women who aren't sluts, that is." Braze pointed his thumb at Bridget. "It took forever to convince this woman that she wanted me."

Bridget smiled and moved to cuddle on his lap. Merco envied the closeness the two of them had.

But what the hell was up with that? He wasn't after a relationship. All he wanted was a good fuck.

"Well, maybe I should apologize to her." He shrugged, standing, knowing he was an unwanted third party there. "That's why I came here anyway. She lives in this building."

Bridget looked up at him, her cheeks glowing while the warmth in her eyes showed she couldn't wait to get back to what she'd been doing before he'd interrupted.

"Oh, does she? What's her name?" she asked.

"She is your good friend, Naomi. I admit being at a loss as to why you two never formally introduced me. She is one hot redhead."

The flash in Bridget's gaze was a warning of her rising temper. "You know better than most that Naomi has been to hell and back. I won't have her enduring anything painful. There is no way she could handle a relationship with you."

"What's wrong with me?" He gave her his best sincere smile, knowing from experience it seldom worked on the stubborn woman.

"I think Bridget feels it's her duty to keep Naomi safe. The poor girl got caught in the grip of the leader of the demons, and ever since we've gotten her back, Bridget protects her."

"Well, I'm not exactly looking for a relationship." Once again, the image of Naomi's sultry body, and that beautiful red hair distracted Merco's thoughts. "I just thought I'd get to know her a bit."

If he hadn't turned his back on Bridget, she never would have been able to send him flying. "You stay the fuck away from her," was all he heard as he was hurled away from the planet.

He slowed himself, allowing the blackness of outer space to absorb around him. Staying away from that redhead was the last thing he planned on doing.

Chapter Three

"I wondered when you would show up." Merco acknowledged the older man who walked through the wall into his bedroom.

"Nice place you have here." Birk, Merco's watcher, stroked his salt-and-pepper beard while taking slow steps toward the bed.

Merco glanced over at the blonde stretching next to him on his bed. He'd intended to fuck the shit out of her, take out all his aggressions in some good, raunchy sex. Looking at her now, her large breasts perfectly shaped, oval nipples all perky, just the way he liked them, and creamy blonde hair that was short and silky, he knew he'd created her because she looked nothing like that blasted redhead.

The redhead who wouldn't stay out of his thoughts, and had been distracting him for well over a week now.

"I'm glad you like it," he muttered.

The blonde opened her eyes, staring up at him with a lazy smile. She would do anything for him. Fuck him any way he wished. She was eager and willing, just like all the other ladies he'd conjured up over the past week. All of them anxious to be his slut, do whatever he wanted.

And the fact that he couldn't get hard for any of them was really starting to piss him off.

"What made you decide to move to Earth?" Birk walked past the bed, ignoring the two of them lying there, and moved to stare out the full-length window. "Nice view you have here," he added conversationally.

"What's wrong with Earth?" Merco looked down the length of the blonde, her smooth mound between her legs nicely tanned.

He wondered if the redhead kept herself shaved.

The blonde rolled into him, her fingers raking through the hair on his chest. She curved one of her legs over his, unconcerned that Birk was in the room. Which didn't surprise him—she had been created to fuck, to give him all that he wanted at the moment.

And at the moment, all he wanted was for her to go away. Waving a hand over her, she disappeared, leaving him feeling as empty as he had when she'd been cuddled into him. Something had to be done. He wasn't accustomed to not getting laid daily, but for the life of him, he couldn't get interested in any of his playmates.

"I've never had a problem with this planet." Birk clasped his hands behind his back, his barrel chest stretching the flannel plaid shirt he wore. Turning, he gave Merco a scrutinizing look. "But from what I hear, you arrive and start trouble immediately."

Merco stood, walking naked over to his full-length mirror. Tall and muscular, he knew he had what any woman craved. But Bridget had given him a firm reminder that Earth women wouldn't just bend over and beg for a good pounding, even if they lusted over you in their mind.

"Good news travels fast." He stared at himself for only a moment in the mirror before dressing.

Faded jeans and a T-shirt would be his attire for the day. He glanced over another second at the image reflecting back at him after making the clothes appear, before turning to Birk.

"I reckon I've allowed myself to get a bit rusty." Merco sighed, running his fingers through his thick hair. "And Bridget is probably right. I shouldn't be messing with the women here."

Birk nodded once, tugging at his beard. "And that is why you've decided to live here."

Birk made a show of looking around the large bedroom, taking a long look out of the tall windows lining the opposite wall. Plush grounds surrounded the home Merco had recently decided to move into. One of the things Merco loved about the place was the wide-open space surrounding the house. When he'd walked around the grounds the first time, imagining a particular redhead strolling over the peaceful surroundings had made him buy it on the spot.

"I've met a lady who intrigues me. I can't help but think about her," he mused, walking over to look out the windows at the land that only urged those thoughts along. "The way Bridget defended her, she must be an incredible person."

Birk chuckled. "I'm impressed. You've never given too much thought to a woman's nature before."

Merco turned around, considering his watcher's words. "Women are treasures, an awesome creation. But the challenge here draws me in."

And that had to be it. No woman for centuries had even considered telling him no. Merco shook his head, his body tightening just thinking of the fire he saw burning in those deep blue eyes of hers.

"What are you going to do?" Birk crossed his large arms over his chest, giving Merco a harsh look. "Bridget monitors this planet with a tight rein. I'm sure she already knows you are here."

Merco waved his hand through the air. Bridget had never been a problem for him. "She is doing a wonderful job of pulling this planet back together. There were so many demons here a person could hardly breathe."

He laughed easily. Braze and Bridget always held a warm spot inside him. They made a wonderful couple and he enjoyed both of them.

"Well, let's just hope she doesn't decide you are one of those demons." Birk didn't smile. The man worried way too much.

"Bridget's concern for the redhead intrigues me. If she has befriended this woman, there must be a quality in her—other than she is damned good-looking—that impresses her." Images of her long braided hair, her creamy skin with those rich blue eyes so full of fire tightened every muscle inside him. This one would be worth the chase. And he had a feeling it would liven his life up a bit to go after such a morsel. "All I have to do is convince Bridget that my intentions are sincere."

Now Birk did laugh. "This will be worth hanging around for."

Merco ignored Birk, his thoughts too consumed by the young woman who had captured his attention unlike any other woman in centuries. Heading toward his bedroom door, he waved a hand in dismissal.

"Pick a room in the house and set up camp if you like," he told his watcher as he headed down the long wide hallway toward the staircase. "I'm going to make a trip into town and do some research."

"Research?" Birk was on his heels.

Merco felt his blood pump through him, enthusiasm mounting while he made a mental plan for his day. How long had it been since he'd set a serious goal, interacted with a woman who wouldn't automatically do his bidding?

"Yup. I'm going to be human for a while, see where it gets me." Merco headed down the stairs and grinned up at his old friend's concerned expression.

Maybe he'd been all about good times for centuries now. But he had to do something about the redhead who wouldn't get out of his thoughts. And taking her on, at her own level, without magic, sounded like an adventure he was anxious to start.

Chapter Four

Working days sucked. After nine years of working third shift, Naomi just couldn't get accustomed to working during the day. Strolling through Westport, the notorious nightlife spot of Kansas City, the thought that she could stop in at one of the clubs, have a drink, and relax after a hard day's work hit her with an awkward realization.

Digging her fists into her coat pockets, she hunched over against a strong icy breeze and kept walking. It would be dark soon, but heading back to her apartment didn't appeal to her tonight. Dreams seemed to haunt her whether she was awake or sleeping. Maybe if she walked herself into a complete state of exhaustion she would be able to just go home and collapse onto her bed without tossing and turning for a change.

Folks at work told her it was normal to endure a sleep adjustment after switching shifts. But for some reason she worried it was more involved than that. Her body burned with a raw ache that seemed to pulse through her with more intensity every day. And her mind crawled with memories she didn't remember having. None of it made any sense.

"Hey, looking good." Several college-age young men sauntered past her, a mixture of leather and beer filling the air around them.

Naomi looked up quickly, her heart suddenly pattering nervously that strangers on the street might flirt with her. In an instant she realized they hadn't spoken to her, but to another lady leaving one of the shops she passed. Diverting her gaze, she hurried along, barely paying attention as she hurried to cross the street.

Men never flirted with her. She just wasn't one of those "stand out in a crowd" type of gals. And with all of her long thick red hair, well she wasn't ashamed that she was a bit plain. Her friends liked her for who she was, not how she looked. Naomi always thought that had given her an advantage over the knockouts.

Another cold wind slapped her cheeks when the row of buildings ended. A chill rushed through her similar to how she had felt the last few nights after waking up.

Night after night, dreams plagued her, of another place, another time, filled with hideous beings she couldn't even begin to describe. Her friend Thena thought maybe there was a spell that would help her. And at this point, she was willing to try anything.

Maybe there was also a spell that would rid her mind of the image of one tall, dark mysterious man who had offered to take all of her aches and cravings away. It wasn't right for him to be so pompous, so damned cocky, and for her to be turned on by it. She wasn't into men like that at all. Nope. No way.

The honking of a car startled her. Naomi almost tripped over her own boots when she looked at the oncoming Jeep speeding straight toward her. Tires made a terrible squealing sound against the paved road. Naomi's heart exploded, her hands going over her face in a futile attempt to block the front end of the car that was approaching her too quickly for her to move.

"No. Oh, God. Please. No." She froze in terror, suddenly shaking so hard that she couldn't move, couldn't run.

She was going to be hit by a car.

Naomi screamed. The sound shocked her. Fire burned through her throat while she yelled in terror, the vehicle coming closer and closer.

In the next instant, a wind rushed around her, hitting her so hard she almost spun in a circle losing her balance. Her hands hit the street, tiny pebbles pinching into her skin. She stopped herself from going to her knees while she struggled to catch her breath.

Strands of hair that would never stay braided fell over her face when she looked up to see the Jeep slow down on the other side of her. An arm waved out the window while the driver yelled something and then the vehicle sped up again.

"Did you see that?" An older man held on to his wife on the other side of the street. "I swear that car drove right through her."

Several others watched while she crossed the street then turned and continued on their way without saying anything. Naomi could hardly walk, her legs shook so hard.

What in the hell had just happened?

Her teeth chattered and the cold seemed to make it hard to stop shaking. If she didn't know better she could have sworn that Jeep drove right through her. After half a block, she ran her hands down her front, making sure she was intact.

Maybe she should just go home. And then maybe she should find a good shrink. Nothing had seemed right lately. With all of her dreams, and meeting that man at the coven meeting the other night, she had been a bit worried about herself. But now, a near-death experience. And she didn't have anyone to talk to about it.

Thena would simply want to mix herbs together. Bridget would reassure her, and she would leave her place feeling calmer. She always felt better after seeing Bridget. But none of that would solve her problems.

Several of the shop signs caught her eye. Maybe buying something trivial and then going home to a hot bath would help.

Across the street, a crystal shop caught her eye. The sign advertised candles and incense. But she would have to cross the street. Naomi took a long look both ways before daring to step foot off of the curb.

Her senses were still quite rattled when she pushed the heavy wooden door open, to be greeted by a rush of warm air and the sweet aroma of a variety of smells. Sage and lavender drifted through the air. It was as if she had entered another world when she let the large door swing silently closed behind her.

A small woman behind the counter looked up and smiled, her gentle blue eyes lighting up at the sight of her.

"Hello, dear," she said, sounding more like a favorite relative welcoming you to her home than a shop owner.

Naomi relaxed a bit, smiling back. She took her time glancing over the items on the shelves, running her fingers over the details of some carved wooden statuettes and noticing some of Bridget's work as well.

"How much is this?" she asked, holding up one of Bridget's candleholders.

The older woman came from around the counter, wearing a long dark skirt that fluttered to her ankles. Soft gray hair had been piled onto her head. Something about the woman made Naomi feel good, at peace. She would have to remember this store for those times when she felt at her wit's end.

Like right now.

"Well, let me see." The shop owner took the metal candleholder, her touch like soft leather when her hand brushed against Naomi's. She ran her fingers over it lovingly as if she'd made it herself. "Oh, yes. That's right. There is a special on these right now. If you buy one of those candles over there, you get this candleholder free."

The woman led Naomi to a stand with several shelves of candles, all different colors and fragrances. The mixed aromas soaked through her, soothing her just like that hot bath she had thought about taking.

"You have quite a selection." She picked up one of the lavender candles and held it to her nose, letting its soft scent trickle through her. Closing her eyes, she swore her muscles relaxed, the stress of her dreams and her almost life-threatening incident seeming to dissipate while she stood there.

"Take your time, my dear. I want to make sure you pick the one just right for you." The shop owner patted her arm and then left her alone.

Naomi definitely needed to make this place a regular stop. A cold wind rattled the windows at the front of the shop, but inside she felt warm and cozy, which was surprising considering how old these downtown buildings were.

"This one would be best for you." The deep voice was barely a whisper over her shoulder.

Naomi turned, startled, and stared into the dark handsome face of the stranger from the coven. A flush of heat spread through her sending her insides burning.

She almost dropped the candle in her hand and he wrapped his fingers around hers, his grip warm and strong.

"I think I can pick out a candle." She managed to sound composed although for the life of her, she couldn't pull her hand away from his.

Nor could she look away from those light green eyes, his dark complexion adding to the intensity of their color. Never had she seen more beautiful eyes on a man. He had long, thick lashes and she imagined from the thickness of his hair that he probably had a chest full of thick dark curls as well.

What the hell was she thinking?

Naomi yanked her hand away from his, once again almost dropping the candle but managing to put it back on the shelf without sending the rest of the candles tumbling on to the floor.

"This one is perfect for you." He reached around her, moving into her space, standing so close to her, the heat from his body scalded her backside.

Her mouth was too dry. Her fingers trembled. It made no sense that a man, just because he was drop-dead gorgeous, would make her react like this.

She stared at the creamy white candle he had picked up off the shelf. His long fingers wrapped around it, holding it in front of her face. She could smell its fragrance without touching it, as well as his musky cologne and rich, all-male scent.

Taking a deep breath she reached for the candle, taking it from him and turning it over to read the name of its fragrance on the label underneath.

You are so beautiful, the label read. She gasped, her breath suddenly staggered as she stared at the simple print and read it again.

"I thought you might believe it more reading it than hearing it from me." His breath tickled the side of her head, sending waves of desire rushing through her.

She turned, her mouth hanging open like a fool. Looking from him to the shop owner behind the counter, she did her best to regain her composure. How in the hell had he managed to have that message under the candle?

Naomi considered herself a levelheaded woman. Very seldom did anyone pull something over on her. Taking a slow cleansing breath, she took a step backwards, running her tongue over her lips. Her mouth was moist for a moment until she realized he watched the small act, then her mouth went dry again while her heart began pounding furiously in her chest.

His hooded gaze, those long eyelashes fluttering over his passionate green eyes, remained focused on her mouth. She swore she wouldn't be able to move until he looked away. It grew harder to breathe, her heart pounding so hard she knew it must be visible through her shirt. She put the candle down, her fingers too damp to continue holding it.

Somehow she managed another step backwards, turning her attention to the store owner, needing someone stable to help bring her thoughts back to a coherent level.

He picked the candle up again. "It is for you," he told her, placing his hand on her back and guiding her toward the counter.

There was no reason to allow him to lead her. Maybe that wasn't the candle that she wanted. Maybe she didn't want to buy anything at all. Dear God. Naomi wished the fog her brain was suddenly in would go away. Her heart raced, blood pumping through her, the need she remembered him promising to take away, hitting her like a brick wall.

"Marlita, wrap these up for her." The man took her candleholder from her and placed the items on the counter.

Marlita, the shop owner, stared at him for only a moment, and then moved her gaze to Naomi. Her expression was relaxed, but there was caution, a sense of concern. If she didn't know better, Naomi would swear the two of them knew each other.

Suddenly the urge to leave this place, this store that had seemed such a sanctuary a moment before, overwhelmed her.

She fumbled for her purse, her fingers trembling. Her wallet seemed too large to get out of her purse.

The man ran his hand down her back, sending chills that did anything but make her cold rushing through her. His fingers pressed against her jacket, his touch searing through the thick material. Her shirt did nothing to block the way he stroked down her, a sensual touch, enticing and controlling. He touched her like he owned her.

And she didn't even know his name.

"Put this on my tab," he told the shop owner, his rich baritone vibrating through her.

Naomi looked up at him quickly, and then diverted her gaze to the woman behind the counter. Just staring at him for the briefest of moments made her insides burn with a need stronger than she could handle. Standing next to him, with his hand on her back, would have her crazy in no time flat.

Marlita's lips turned up at the corners, a small reassuring smile. Her gaze was so warm, stable and relaxing, just like this shop.

She patted Naomi's hand, her touch cool, soothing against the fire burning inside her. "Enjoy the candle, my dear."

Naomi thanked her, mumbling the words the best she could, her mouth suddenly too dry. Walking home would do her some good. All she had to do was get out of this shop, and away from this tall, sensual stranger.

It entered her head that she shouldn't hurry out of the store so quickly. She should be grateful for the gift, offer a parting smile or something. But if she turned to look at him, if she so much as allowed him to seep through her senses any further, she would be lost, a complete puddle on the floor.

There was no reason at all why someone who had been so arrogant, so pompous, so presumptuous, should be turning her insides into pure jelly. And that was exactly what he was doing.

She glanced at the items on the shelves around her while she headed toward the large wooden door. Something on display caught her attention. A variety of ceramic items cluttered a table, but this item stood out.

A tall, intricately detailed statuette looked up at her from the front of the display. A hideous creature, distorted and gaunt, his back hunched and his head too large for his body, seemed to glare at her.

Naomi's breath caught in her throat as she froze, staring at the ugly thing. She couldn't look away. It was impossible that this tiny ceramic thing matched the god-awful creature in her dreams.

Images appeared in her mind. Grotesque memories that haunted her dreams every night. Suddenly she couldn't breathe. Everything closed in around her while the room began to spin.

"Naomi. Sweetheart, are you okay?" Strong hands gripped her arms, stabilizing her, although her heart still raced.

All she could do was point at the terrible statuette, feeling like a fool while her breathing came in erratic gasps.

He pulled her against him while reaching down and grabbing the nasty-looking thing. For a moment Naomi had a terrible image of the hideous creature coming to life, struggling against the grip.

"Marlita!" His voice bellowed over her head with such ferocity that she jumped in his arms. He turned her when he moved to face the shopkeeper. "Why, in the name of all the gods, would you have this in here?"

"Merco. I swear." Marlita's hands went to her mouth, her expression growing as pale as Naomi felt. "I have no idea how that got there."

Naomi screamed when he crushed the statuette in his hand, the hideous thing turning to dust—dust that disappeared before it hit the floor.

"Oh, my God," she cried out.

Strong arms wrapped around her, the warmth from his body wrapping around her when he pulled her close to him.

"Where…where did it go?" A ringing started in her ears. She'd never passed out in her entire life, but almost felt it might be a nice escape from this sudden nightmare.

The only difference between right now and her dreams was this tall dark stranger—had the owner of the store called him Merco? Hard muscles, the epitome of male perfection, held her close—too damned close. Fear and desire rushed through her, torturing her senses, making it impossible to think straight. A tremble crept over her, chilling her against the heat of his body. Not once in her life had she experienced such a turmoil of emotions. She would lose her mind at this rate. There were no doubts on that one.

"I swear to you that he will never bother you again." Merco's breath was warm against her cheek, but the kiss he planted on her cheek after he spoke scalded her skin.

And her brain. And her body, sending heat straight to her pussy, which began to throb with an ache she feared would get her in trouble. She wasn't thinking clearly enough at the moment to be surrounded by such intense sexuality. And this man brimmed over with it.

"You would have to be in my dreams to accomplish that," she mumbled, heat burning her cheeks the minute she spoke. What in the hell did she say something like that for?

"That can be arranged," he told her, and for some reason, she really believed that he meant that.

Chapter Five

He could take her anywhere right now and fuck the shit out of her. And normally that is exactly what he would do, deciding the distraction would be best for her.

But as he looked over at Marlita, the watcher eyeing both of them with concern in her eyes, he wondered at the compassion he felt for this frail human.

Bridget had seen to Naomi forgetting all about the terrible experience she had endured in the hells. For some reason though, Naomi hadn't completely forgotten about it.

Looking over her head at Marlita, he knew Bridget's watcher would contact her the moment he left. With Naomi in his arms like this, her soft body pressed so closely to his, her sensual curves bringing out a protector's instinct he hadn't felt in quite a while, he knew he would endure Bridget's wrath to ensure Naomi's protection.

And she needed to be protected.

"I'm taking you home." He looked down at her long red hair, parted neatly in the middle of her head.

He wouldn't think right now of how beautiful she would look with her braids undone, with those long locks draping over her curvy body. Dwelling on how soft her ass was pressed against him, and how it would look with her on her knees, his hands kneading her flesh, was not where his thoughts needed to be right now.

Marlita opened her mouth to speak, but he silenced her. Naomi didn't need to hear anymore. He wouldn't have Bridget's watcher saying anything that would alarm her further. Marlita accepted the silent order, shutting her mouth and then running her tongue over her lips slowly. She would alert Bridget. But that didn't bother him.

Naomi needed him. That realization sent a fire rushing through him, hardening him with the need to protect her. He couldn't remember the last time he'd felt this way. There would be no more dreams, none at least that would traumatize her. No one would stop him from protecting her.

He had her through the door, the cold night air doing nothing to calm the fury that burned through him, before she said anything.

"I don't need an escort home. I'm fine." She looked up at him with soft blue eyes filled with curiosity and confusion.

He didn't see any of the fear within her anymore. She brushed her tongue against her top lip, her mouth parting ever so slightly with the action. Watching her small hand reach up to smooth her hair, he didn't miss the slight tremble in her fingers. She hid her fear well, but her actions betrayed her thoughts.

"You want to walk home in the cold and the dark?" He couldn't keep his hands off of her. Running his fingers over her red hair, he fought the urge to undo the braids right there on the spot. He was up for the challenge of persuading her with his charm, instead of his powers. "Your chariot awaits you, my dear."

Naomi turned when he gestured and looked at the street where a shiny black Corvette waited for them. Its motor hummed, inviting them into the intimate warmth of its cozy interior.

Merco stepped around her, opening the car door. Her caution spawned yet another unfamiliar emotion that hardened his insides and rushed rabidly through his tortured system. She studied the purring machine only for a moment, and then her gaze darted to him, scanning him quickly before looking at the car again.

"Material possessions don't impress me," she told him, her adorable nose going up in the air while she gave him a haughty stare.

"I'll remember that," he told her, noticing how the cold had hardened her nipples into tiny beacons. They pressed against the material of her shirt, which already stretched over her full round breasts.

Naomi's cheeks flushed a delightful red, bringing out the blue in her eyes. She ran her tongue over her lips before sucking in a breath. Her shirt stretched even more over her breasts, sending a rush of heat straight to Merco's cock. Suddenly his human body no longer felt the cold. Instead fire burned through him. The urge to throw her over his shoulder and disappear to a much more intimate setting overwhelming him.

This playing human was a pain in the ass. All this pretense. He wanted one thing—to see her spread beneath him, her body arched with pleasure while she screamed through her orgasm. He wanted to fuck her silly.

"Good." She moved quickly, bending over and sliding into the passenger seat.

Oh, hell, yeah. What he wouldn't do to spread that ass wide open, devour her. And it would all be so easy if he just used his powers. Playing this game of being human was starting to be hard work.

When he climbed in on the other side, she didn't look at him, but wrapped her arms around her chest, as if she were still cold. The warm interior of the car made it hard to see out of the windows. Looking down, he took in the complex console and the many buttons and levers. Pushing his foot on the long pedal, the engine revved, but the car didn't move. Maybe he should just make it drive itself. That would be a lot easier. He didn't have a clue how to drive the thing.

"The brake is on," she said without looking at him.

Her small fingers tapped an extended lever in between them that stuck out like his cock would if it weren't confined in his pants.

The last thing he would do would be to embarrass himself in front of this sexy woman. He had her so close, willing to go with him, and he wouldn't ruin it by frightening her with his lack of earthly knowledge.

"Engines like this are very delicate. They need to be prepared." Immediately he sensed amusement fill the small confines of the car. This wasn't going the way he wanted it to. Once again he thought of simply taking her away somewhere, dipping into her fruits and feasting until he was full.

He could make her want him. Altering her perception of him just a bit would have her begging him to do whatever he wanted. It would take such little effort.

But he would see this challenge through, damn it. Too many centuries had passed since he'd allowed any woman in his presence free will. His own creations, his own sluts, begged to do anything he wished to them. Tasting Naomi, once she offered herself to him without fight, would be worth all the minor embarrassments he might have to endure to get there.

Releasing the brake didn't do anything. The car sat there, humming quietly, its soft vibrations underneath them doing nothing to help him understand its mechanism. Maybe if he'd taken time to do more driving, partake in the activities of the mortals scattered across the planets, this machine would make sense to him. Most of their contraptions seemed to be similar regardless of the planet. After all, they all stemmed from the same seeds.

He would have to wing it. Gripping the handle next to the wheel in front of him, he pulled on it, there not being anything else on the console in front of him to grab. Instantly the car rolled forward. Easy enough. He pushed the pedal with his foot, and the thing roared to life. Immediately other cars around him began honking.

"When's the last time you drove this thing?" Naomi grabbed the handle next to her with one hand and braced herself against the dash with the other.

He looked at her. Her eyes were wide with fright. Blood pumped through her veins at an accelerated rate, her heart pounding too hard in her chest. She was a fragile creature, so delicate, yet determined to act so strong. For a moment, he couldn't look away, but simply feasted on her beauty, those full red lips, her creamy white skin, and that gorgeous red hair that really needed to be set free, allowed to stream around her without constraint. She was more perfect than any woman he'd ever created.

"Usually I don't drive." There was no need to offer further explanation. Better to be a mystery, than for her to know the truth.

In time, after he'd fucked her, and if she proved worth keeping around for a while, he would let her know of his powers. But until then, it was best to keep her in the dark.

"I can tell." She sounded disgusted. Her amused attitude was gone.

Merco frowned, an uncomfortable emotion washing through him that he wasn't accustomed to feeling. The thought that she wouldn't like him had never crossed his mind. And he didn't like the idea now. Gripping the steering wheel, he focused on the road in front of them, trying to make sure the car did what he wanted it to. "Tell me how to get to your home."

Letting her know he'd already been to her apartment building would be a fool's mission. Once he had her trust, fucking her would be no problem.

"The first thing you need to do is turn around. You're going in the wrong direction." She had reached to pull a strap around her, fastening it next to her hip.

She wasn't amused, hesitation ringing in her voice. He was losing points by the second. Fucking sluts of his own creation was a hell of a lot easier than trying to get someone to like him first—and without using any powers. He wondered for a second if this was worth it. His cock burned with a fire more intense than he'd known for centuries. Blood rushed through his human body, burning him with a dangerous craving.

"Okay. We'll turn around." He forced himself to focus on the street around him, which was full of cars. Concentrating on anything other than those soft curves, those delicate hands, the way she licked her lips when she was nervous, hurt his brain.

He'd made a deal with himself not to use magic on her. Allowing her time to want him, to beg for him to appease the craving he knew burned wildly inside her would be worth his own torment. However that didn't mean he couldn't alter the world around him.

With a thought, the cars on the road disappeared, making it easy to turn the car around.

"What in the hell are you doing?" she shrieked, grabbing his arm with a strength he didn't realize she had.

Straightening the car out so that he was now going in the opposite direction, he gave her his attention. Her mouth hung open, perfectly shaped for his cock. Her eyes were wide, a fiery blue that enticed him. Such energy. Such spirit.

"Let me out of this car, right-fucking-now!" she screamed at him, and at the same time grabbed the door handle.

"You're not going to leave me." It was a simple fact. He would see this to the end. And he would say when that was, not Naomi. She would see that making demands of him, especially ridiculous demands, weren't to her advantage. "Are you in that big of a rush to get home so that demon can haunt you some more?"

All color washed from her face. She stared at him for a moment, not blinking, but fear wrapped around her like a thick blanket. He watched her lips start to tremble.

"I want out of the car now. Please." Her voice cracked as she spoke.

"Naomi." He kept his voice calm, reassuring. What mattered now was that she calm down. His gut turned at the thought that he could fail with her before he'd had a chance to even get started. "There are things about me that you don't know. Many things. But what you do need to know is that you can trust me. I will never hurt you."

Her expression didn't change. "Well, there is something that I know about you. You don't know how to drive. Now pull over before you get us both killed."

He brought the car to the side of the road and put his foot on the pedal that stopped the car. The thing jerked to a stop.

"Ow!" she cried out again, her body smashing forward against the strap that restrained her. "Maybe you wouldn't intentionally hurt me. But trust you? Not as far as I could throw you."

She jumped out of the car, and marched down the sidewalk, her braids swaying against her back.

"Damn." Merco jumped out as well, waving his hand at the car so that it disappeared.

The fool woman was determined to walk home. She wouldn't walk away from him though. Picking up pace, he stayed behind her, the smooth sway of her hips so tantalizing his mouth watered.

She would be his. Just the thought of capturing her passion, pinning down her lust so that no man would satisfy her other than him, made his cock swell while his heart beat too fast.

Her legs were shorter than his, but keeping up with her was physically painful when he ached with a fiery passion throughout his entire body. When her apartment complex was in sight across the street she slowed, looking over her shoulder.

"Why are you following me?" she asked, turning to glance both ways carefully before entering the street.

He fell into stride next to her. "I'm not letting you walk home alone."

"I don't need a bodyguard." She brushed her braid over her shoulder, walking around the parked cars in her parking lot as she headed toward the glass doors of her complex.

"You need more than a bodyguard." He grabbed her when she reached the entrance of her complex. There was no way he would let her go that easily.

He took her arm and she turned on him quickly. Her free hand raised, as if she would slap him, and he grabbed it. Pinning her hands behind her back, he crushed her to him.

There was no hesitation. The need in him had grown too strong. He kissed her.

And the fire from her mouth almost made him melt. Her body was stiff, not fighting him, but not relaxing. But she didn't move. She didn't pull away from him.

He ran his tongue over her lips, felt their softness, their fullness, tasted her.

When a moment passed and she did nothing to make him stop, he tightened his grip around her, running his hand up the narrow curve of her back and tangling his fingers in her hair.

Arching her head back, he pressed his tongue through her slightly parted lips. She opened them further on a gasp. She wanted him. She craved him with the same intensity that he craved her, and that pushed him forward. A growl escaped him when he entered her mouth. Her heat, her own unique taste, her hesitant submission, was a drug that coursed through his body, attacking his system and making him want her more than he remembered ever wanting another woman.

She turned her head slightly, forcing their mouths away.

"Please," she gasped, her body relaxing against his while she struggled for breath.

"Yes?" he whispered against her cheek, while applying moist kisses against her soft skin.

He worked his way to her ear then sucked the soft flesh into his mouth. "Tell me what you want."

He wanted to hear her voice her thoughts, confess that she yearned for him to be buried deep inside her.

A soft tap on his shoulder grabbed his attention. Someone tried to steal his thoughts with a finger poking his shoulder. He didn't bother to stop what he was doing. There was no reason to turn and see who might be standing behind him. Already he knew there was no one there. The soft tap was a reminder. A gentle way of letting him know that he wasn't pleasing someone.

"I want..." Naomi sucked in a breath, pressing her hands against his chest and giving a slight push. "I need to go inside."

He let her move to arm's reach but kept her in his embrace, looking down at her. Naomi didn't look up but apparently focused on her hands. He caressed her arms, enjoying the soft touch of her. Her fingers spread across his chest, covering his heart, soaking him with her warm touch.

He couldn't remember the last time he'd seen such incredible natural beauty. Usually he preferred his women with lots of makeup, bright red lipstick, long thick lashes. But Naomi didn't need any of it. The way loose strands waved around her face, refusing to stay bound, the soft cream color of her skin, her full lips, the gleam of hesitation warring in her expression. He knew beyond a doubt that no one would keep her from him.

"You need to be with me." And he knew by the way she stayed in his arms that she wanted to be with him. He didn't even need to read her thoughts to know that much.

But then she pushed harder against his chest, taking a step back. He let go of her but didn't move, the space between them a burning inferno of lust. Sparks burst inside him, his need rupturing while the ache became almost unbearable.

"Why do you say that? You don't even know me." She crossed her arms over her chest, looking over her shoulder as if she wanted to turn to go inside but her own desires prevented her from moving.

Her body language spoke volumes. This woman craved him possibly more than any woman had ever wanted him.

"I know you are searching, that what you live with right now isn't acceptable." He caught her chin in his hand, lifting her face to his. The soft glow of her blue eyes was like a pool that he could swim in forever. "You do need me."

"I've got to go," she whispered, her lips trembling until she sucked them in, running her tongue over them.

"All you have to do is think about me, and I'll be there." He took a step back, hating to do so, knowing he would suffer incredibly until he saw her again.

Chapter Six

Naomi was surprised to see Bridget standing just inside the foyer when she entered the dimly lit complex. The familiar damp smell of what had been her home now for several years welcomed her, along with Bridget's concerned look.

"Are you okay?" Bridget looked past her toward the doors, then focused on Naomi's flushed expression.

She was sure her friend saw straight through her, to the burning desire that still smoldered inside her from Merco's kiss.

"I'm fine. What are you doing down here?" Naomi asked, hoping she sounded relaxed and assuring.

Her heart beat a mile a minute, and she swore it was warmer in the building than usual.

"Just checking mail." Bridget smiled and turned for the stairwell, her concern turning amiable. "So what did you do tonight?"

"I went downtown." They climbed the stairs side by side.

Naomi had a feeling that her friend wanted more details, but she just didn't feel like sharing anything about Merco. She didn't understand the man herself. How could she explain him to Bridget?

They stopped in front of Naomi's apartment. Bridget's was just down the hall, the door slightly ajar with a dim light glowing from inside.

"Naomi. There is something I need to say." Bridget put her hand on Naomi's arm, a friendly gesture but for some reason it sent nervous prickles down Naomi's spine. Bridget smiled reassuringly. "The man you were with outside, Merco. He isn't right for you."

"You know Merco?" Naomi might actually get some answers about the mysterious man. Immediately she had hundreds of questions she wanted to ask Bridget about him. "Is he married?" she began, asking the big one first.

Bridget shook her head. "Merco isn't marrying material," she said, her expression turning serious. "Naomi. You are my friend, my dear friend. And I would cry if anyone ever hurt you. Please promise me. Stay away from him."

Naomi hadn't decided if she wanted to see him again or not. But being told not to didn't sit well with her. If anyone other than Bridget had said that to her, she would have told them to fuck off.

"Is there something wrong with him?" she asked, fearing the worse.

Wouldn't it just be her luck for the most gorgeous man in town to be pursuing her, and he had some fatal disease.

Bridget shook her head. "Nothing like that. It's just that, well, Merco has a very unique sex drive…to say the least," she added under her breath. "Just promise me you will stay away from him. I don't want you hurt."

Naomi didn't know what to say. Of course her best friend would know that she wasn't very sexually active. Hell, she hadn't been with a man in ages. But it wasn't because she didn't like sex. She loved sex. There just weren't that many men out there who didn't turn out to be real jerks after the first date.

She mumbled something that she was sure was incoherent and turned toward her door, entering her dark empty apartment. There was no reason to turn on the lights. She was numb as she walked through her living room into her bedroom and reached for the small lamp next to her bed. She plopped down on the edge of the bed. There was no way she would be able to fall asleep now.

It turned out falling asleep wasn't the problem. The dreams that haunted her were worse than if she hadn't been able to sleep. Naomi kicked her blankets off of her, unable to wake up as the voices tormented her, the visions in front of her terrifying her.

"Come to me, you little slut." The grotesque creature moved with lazy confidence, his grayish-green eyes too moist while he ogled her. "You will never escape me, never be free of me. You are mine to enjoy for eternity. No one will stop me when I exist in your mind."

She tried to cry out, to scream, to move her hands so that she could strike him, or prevent him from touching her. For some reason she couldn't move. She couldn't speak.

Heat burned through her as if flames danced around her, torturing her. Everything around her was dark. The dampness in the air saturated her clothing, giving her a chill even though she sweltered from the suffocating heat.

If only she could tell him no, tell him to go away, to get his bony fingers off of her.

The stench of the creature surrounded her, his heavy breathing showing how excited he was. Moisture clung to her skin where he touched her, his clammy hands giving her nasty chills even though she sweated from overwhelming heat and humidity.

"You can't fight me. You don't have the strength." His hissing laughter as he groped at her, fondled her breasts, tugged at her clothes, made her want to puke.

She shook her head frantically, tears staining her eyes. Her hair stuck to her face, blinding her as strands stuck to the salty moisture that streamed to her mouth. If only she could scream, call out, someone – anyone.

Try as she would, her mouth wouldn't open. Her lips seemed sealed shut, her tears clinging to her mouth while she strained to speak, tell the hideous creature that now mauled at her breasts to leave her alone, get out of her head.

I won't submit to you, not now, not ever, *she screamed in her thoughts, her throat aching even though she hadn't voiced her words.*

"You already have." It read her thoughts, swimming through her mind as if it were his personal playground. "I can play with you, torture you, enjoy your screams. Nothing you can do will ever change that. No one can stop me. You'll see to it."

His laughter curled her blood, tearing through her with vicious claws.

Her tongue was stuck to the top of her mouth. She fought to make her mouth work, to voice her pleas, beg the cruel beast to leave her alone.

"No!" She screamed, struggling with the blankets cocooned around her as she flew out of her bed and fell to the floor.

Naomi stood quickly, the blankets flowing off the bed while she hurried to her bedroom door. She breathed quickly, gulping in air, while staring at her quiet, dark room. Struggling to straighten her oversized T-shirt that she always slept in, she stared frantically into the darkness.

Everything was in place. It was just another dream.

"And I'm sick of them," she mumbled, tearing her fingers through her knotted hair.

She hadn't bothered to take her hair out of her braids before bed. Now her fingers shook while she unwrapped her long locks of hair. It fell around her, a cloak to hide behind. Yet this time, the scary creature was in her head, not in a closet, or the adjoining dark room. There was no way to hide from her thoughts.

Her heart raced. A cold sweat had spread over her body, and she fought off uncontrollable shivers. There was nothing to be scared of. Dreams were just the product of an overactive imagination.

Nonetheless, her knees wobbled as she left her bedroom and headed to her kitchen. The glow of the refrigerator offered a bit of normalcy to her frazzled brain. She needed to calm down, get that stupid creature out of her thoughts so she could go back to sleep.

"Merco, could you chase my dreams away?" She closed her refrigerator, nothing in there appealing to her, and turned to stand in her kitchen doorway.

A different kind of chill ran through her at the thought of the tall, determined stranger. Something about him, his determination, his overwhelming self-confidence, or maybe his dark, forbidding good looks, made her breath almost come in pants.

"You said you would come to me if I needed you." She allowed a smile. At this rate she would truly be insane. Like whispering out loud her desire for a man would bring him to her.

"And I meant it." His deep voice behind her, whispering the simple sentence, broke the silence of her small apartment.

Naomi's heart exploded. She whirled around, almost falling into the refrigerator.

"What the fuck? How'd you get in here?" She stared in horrified disbelief at the man standing in front of her.

Then she let her gaze travel down him. Any thoughts of bad dreams vanished in an instant. Merco stood less than a foot from her, in the doorway, wearing nothing more than cream-colored boxer shorts. He didn't even have on socks.

She focused on his feet for only a moment, her gaze traveling slowly up him. Cords of muscles twisted under dark skin. Black hairs coursed over his body, making her skin tingle even though she hadn't touched him. But when she got to his waist, her mouth went dry, then suddenly was too moist. No man had ever made ordinary boxer shorts look so damn good.

The outline of his shaft, long and thick, in what she hoped wasn't too relaxed of a state, because he was more than well-endowed, was clearly visible through his boxers. The round bulging head of his cock pressed against the material, right under his waistline.

The man stood too close, taking up her space. She couldn't help but stare at him, but hell, she couldn't breathe. And she sure as hell couldn't say anything.

Daring to enjoy the eye candy in front of her, her gaze strolled up his chest, broad thick muscles bulging under skin she ached to touch. She almost gasped for air when she looked him in the face, his green eyes sensual pools clear enough to allow her to see the extent of his desires.

He reached for her, wrapping several strands of her unbrushed hair through his fingers. With a gentle tug, he brought her closer to him. "Did you let your hair down of your own free will?"

What a preposterous question. "No. The demon in my head made me do it."

She frowned at the curious expression that crossed his face, and immediately regretted her smartass remark.

Pulling her hair free from his grasp, she turned around quickly. He was too much man, taking up too much of her personal space. Naomi didn't need this right now. She walked over to her sink, grabbing the cool porcelain, willing it to be enough to calm her frazzled nerves. First that damned recurring nightmare, and now Merco. She couldn't handle this.

"How the hell did you get in here?" She knew she'd locked her front door.

Trying desperately to remember everything she did before she went to bed proved fruitless. Her mind was in a state of pure chaos. And Merco standing behind her wasn't helping a bit.

"I told you that if you called for me I would be here." He moved behind her, pressing his body against her backside.

Naomi couldn't catch her breath. She stared down as her knuckles went white, gripping the counter while her fingers pressed against the sink. Long red hair fell in ringlets, hiding her, allowing her a little privacy while her heart pounded in her chest. It would be too easy to put aside her personal torturous dreams and allow this man to seduce her. He wanted to fuck her. Maybe a quick lay with a perfect stranger would offer her a good night's sleep. God knows she hadn't had one in ages.

"I didn't call you." Hell, she didn't even know his number.

But that was what he had said. And he hadn't offered his number. It was as if all she had to do was whisper her craving for him and he would appear to take care of her.

Good God. Maybe she was still dreaming.

"Yes. You did." He ran his hands up her arms, long fingers stretching underneath her sleeves, pushing her T-shirt to her shoulders. "What demon haunts your dreams?"

"Don't worry about it." The last thing she could do was talk about it.

Especially when his fingers branded her skin. His touch was too hot. For a moment thoughts of the too humid heat in her nightmare grabbed her, attacking her senses. She shuddered. But she wasn't cold. Merco's touch sent smoldering flames through her, but it was far from unpleasant.

"As long as you agree not to worry about it either." He pressed his head against the side of her face, his breath carrying a minty aroma to it.

If Merco was a drug, she could easily become addicted. And drugs were bad. She shouldn't allow this to happen. And she knew exactly where this was headed. Her body screamed in torment, her breasts swelling, feeling suddenly too heavy. She willed him to move his hands, grab hold of them and squeeze. Her nipples burned with a craving to be sucked, tugged on and nibbled.

"I'm not agreeing to anything." She hated how her words escaped her mouth on a breath, sounding way too sensual.

Merco chuckled, the deep baritone sound rippling through her like waves slapping up against a parched beach. She craved him just as dry land craved water. Something was seriously wrong here.

She should be concerned about how he got into her apartment. Merco was a cocky, arrogant cuss, his attitude way too sure of himself, his abilities way too crafted. If she were in her right mind, he would terrify her more than her dream had.

Merco let his fingers trace fiery lines over her shoulders. He ran his hands over her shirt, cupping her neck and stretching it, forcing her head back with his fingers.

Damn. If the iron body pressed against her backside was any indication of how strong he was, he could snap her neck easily. And she didn't know this man at all. Her best friend had warned her to steer clear. Bridget hadn't elaborated on the type of sexual adventures that Merco indulged in. But sneaking into a woman's house, and then holding her neck so that she could hardly move, might put him in a category that Naomi should run from.

"I would never do anything you didn't want." He seemed able to read her mind.

His hot whisper brushed over her cheek, sending her brain into a fever that had her spinning.

"But I will do everything you ache for, what you crave, what you need," he added, his lips brushing over hers.

She opened her mouth to speak, staring into those deep green orbs that were more than hypnotic. Her pussy convulsed, too vulnerable under the simple fabric that hung barely to her thighs. Stretching her back like this, arching her neck so that she looked up at him, her nipples pressed against her shirt, while moisture soaked her inner thighs, her clit pulsating in a beat that matched the rapid beat of her heart.

When she would have spoken, although for the life of her she had no idea what to say, he pressed his mouth over hers, capturing her breath in a kiss that made her explode inside. His lips were soft, but his actions determined. His tongue dipped deep into her mouth, swirling around her, filling her the way she knew his cock would fill her pussy.

She couldn't breathe. Couldn't think. Her mind burned with a feverish need, responding to the throbbing ache that made her want to press her hands over her own heat, soothe the need that burned out of control between her legs.

His fingers stretched along the width of her neck, holding her head in place. His touch was gentle yet intoxicating. He barely touched her, making no effort to explore her exposed and vulnerable body. And damn it to hell if she didn't want him to. In fact, she begged in her mind for his hands to stroke her, fondle her breasts, reach down and penetrate her with those strong fingers.

The reality that she had tangled with insanity made her wonder if she'd truly gone over the edge. Maybe her nightmares were simply proof that her mind had somehow cracked.

Merco had broken into her apartment. He was taking advantage of her when she was at her most vulnerable. It was the middle of the night. And she barely knew the man. And proof of her insanity was the fact that on the edge of her tongue, she was about ready to ask him to fuck her.

His tongue warred with hers. A dance of enticement, him on the sexual prowl and her on the verge of explosion. There was no way she could turn him away, tell him no, make him leave.

His fingers caressed her neck, such strength coated with a soft sensual touch. Her pussy throbbed, the heat between her legs unbearable. She opened her mouth further, allowing him to turn her head with the slightest of touches against her throat.

Never had she tasted such heat, Merco giving her more than she possibly imagined a kiss could do.

Somehow she had to regain control of her senses. If she only could find the strength to end this kiss.

Merco allowed their lips to part, leaving her gasping when he trailed his hot mouth over her cheek to her ear. His body was harder than steel, pressing against her back. The urge to rub her ass against him, entice him further, entered her mind.

Yup. She was surely insane.

"Is this really all you want from me?" he asked, whispering in her ear with such a soothing baritone that chills raced through her straight to her toes. "A mere kiss and you feel you can't handle any more?"

She almost took the challenge. Heat swarmed through her, electric currents tingling every nerve ending in her body. It was as if her world around her, her very own kitchen, the hard counter pressing against her waist, all of it seemed to be the dream. The only reality was Merco. His strength, his passion rushing through her at a speed fast enough to leave her spinning, made everything else in her world seem surreal. And it just seemed natural to respond, to tell him she could handle anything he could give her, she needed everything he had.

Gulping in air, her heart pounding so hard that it hurt, Naomi pushed away from the counter, pressing even harder against the steel body behind her. She would die. She would absolutely die. No woman in her right mind would decline such an offer.

But hadn't she just confirmed that she was surely going insane?

"You broke into my home." Her body clenched with frustration as she forced herself to face the truth.

More than anything she wanted to give in to this man. Her pussy throbbed desperately, moisture warring with the cool air that fluttered underneath her long T-shirt.

She gritted her teeth, fighting to keep her thoughts straight. "I don't know how you got in here, but it isn't right."

"You wanted me." His words brushed over her skin, his hands leaving her neck and stroking her arms. "And you knew calling me would bring me here."

She couldn't fight him when he wrapped his arms around her waist, spreading his fingers over her abdomen. The fire from his touch immobilized her, stealing her breath, making it impossible to move.

"Let me in, darling," he whispered, his head leaning forward next to hers.

She knew he looked down her front and she imagined his view, unable to move her head, lower her eyes, or even think. The way his chest pressed against her shoulder blades, his taut abdomen brushing against the narrow of her back, and his hard cock, stirring with raging fire along her lower back, she was lucky she didn't puddle at his feet.

He would see her breasts, swollen and aching to be caressed. Her heart pounded in her chest and she was certain he noticed how heavily she breathed. And the way she gripped the counter, unable to let go from its solid reassurance that something stable existed in her world, he would know she was on the verge of begging him to fuck her.

"Tell me that you want me," he added, his hoarse whisper rupturing her senses.

Somehow she managed to move her mouth, her own voice no more than a husky breath. "Do I have a choice?"

Chapter Seven

Merco's insides hardened with her words.

Did she have a choice?

He had used no magic. There were no ancient spells at play here. In all the ways he remembered, he was behaving as any human man would behave. Yet still, she claimed that she had no free will.

"You have a choice. Tell me to go away. Or tell me to stay with you." Never had he craved a woman the way he did Naomi.

The way he had her pinned to her counter, her long, thick, dark red hair streaming around her, teasing his skin where it gently floated over him, was enough to make him want to fuck her silly.

But there was more to it than that. Naomi craved him with every breath she took. Her breasts swelled, her nipples poking defiantly against her T-shirt, her scent taking on a musky aroma, proof that she craved him with a lust bordering on something darker, more energized than he had experienced in centuries. No woman he'd ever created had shown him such raw desire, such intense emotions.

Yet Naomi denied those emotions. And worse yet, buried underneath her riveting passion lay something intense, something dark and terrifying to her. She had called out to him for protection. But at the same time, she feared him.

She pushed harder against him, freeing herself from where he had her pinned. It took some effort to let her go, watch her flee into the darkness of her living room. When she turned, her blue eyes glowed against her flushed cheeks. The soft waves in her hair simply added to her incredible beauty. Standing there facing him, her shirt long enough to just cover the treasure between her legs, she nibbled her lower lip, fighting her desire to run back to him. Her thoughts were as easy to read as if she spoke them aloud.

"You act like the only matter at hand here is whether you fuck me or not." She put her hands on her hips, causing her shirt to rise up slightly, her slender legs exposed clear up to her thighs. "What really matters is how the fuck you got into my apartment."

He moved in on her slowly, enjoying how her eyes widened but she held her stance. She had no idea what she dealt with in him, and although her fear was clearly readable, she stood up to him, not backing down for an instant.

"If that is what matters to you so much," he began, keeping his voice low, soft, not wanting to alarm her, and needing her to see she was safe only with him, "then know now that whenever you are in trouble, or simply wish for me to be there, a mere thought will bring me to you. Is that clear?"

"Clear as mud," she mumbled, her pouting expression showing she wouldn't push him further on the matter but her curiosity was more than piqued.

He couldn't keep from touching her, running his thumb over those pursed lips. Everything inside him hardened, stealing his breath momentarily as he stared into her deep blue pools of passion.

"Don't fear me, Naomi," he whispered.

"I don't." Her breath was hot against his fingers, rushing through him with an energy that blinded him.

And the terror he'd read all over her when he first came to her had dissipated. She was leery of him, hesitating, but a craving that almost surpassed his own radiated from her. His cock burned as he fought the urge to rip her shirt from her body, bend her over right there in her living room, and dive into her heat.

He gripped her chin, lifting her face until his was inches from hers. "Tell me what you want."

Her lips parted, her request right there, yet she hesitated. "I…I want…" she stammered, unable to voice her desires as her lashes fluttered over her pretty blue eyes.

"Yes?" He would wait an eternity to hear her say she wanted him to fuck her.

It might kill him to do it, but he was determined now. If he could just ignore the pain that hardened his entire body, demanding that he free his cock from the burden of his clothing.

"You are cornering me. That isn't fair." She nibbled on her lower lip, her lashes fluttering over her eyes until she dared to look at him, their color having darkened to the shade of a stormy sky. "I won't be coerced into anything when you refuse to answer a simple question."

A simple question. She had no clue how complicated the answer would be. Telling her that he simply appeared when she thought of him would confuse her even further. And it had nothing to do with the matter at hand.

"Naomi." He reached for her shoulders.

She didn't pull away from him nor did she look away. Her wide-eyed expression as her hair traipsed over his hands and down her back made her almost appear vulnerable. He doubted, if anything, that she was that.

Letting his hands slide past the material of her shirt and over her arms, the softness of her skin entranced him. What he wouldn't do to run his hands over her entire body, feel her under his touch, adore her beauty.

He took her hands in his. "All that matters is that you want me. And I want you."

Her hands were limp in his, soft and warm, her fingers barely pressing against his skin. He pulled her fingers to his pants, placing her palms over his bulging shaft. Her face lowered, watching the movement, but she didn't pull away. She didn't shy from his efforts.

When her fingers spread over the length of his cock, Merco thought he would explode right there. A groan escaped his throat, the heat from her touch rushing through him, his blood boiling through him savagely.

"Naomi," he growled, barely able to focus on her curious fingers as she explored his cock through his boxers.

"And you say you aren't dangerous," she breathed, then slowly looked up at him.

The thunderstorm had left her eyes. Now a glassy, brilliant blue, full of passion and curiosity. Her lips were moist, full, forming an adorable circle that he would love to shove his cock through.

She was messing with fire. Her teasing would put him over the edge. There was no way he could be responsible for his actions if she didn't stop immediately. And he should tell her that. Warn her.

"I guess that depends on what you are afraid of," he told her.

For a moment, a dark shadow passed over her gaze, something sinister, but then it was gone. She licked her lips slowly, lust consuming her. He didn't miss the hidden fear, the suppressed terror that had forced her to call out to him. Something plagued her that had forced her to cry out to him for help. He would discover what ate at her, the source of the cloud that had briefly dimmed her pretty eyes.

Without warning she pressed her fingers around his swollen shaft. Blood rushed to the head of his cock, the pressure stealing his breath. He sucked in air through his teeth.

"This doesn't scare me." She was about to squeeze the life out of him.

When she let go he almost felt lightheaded. Turning from him she moved toward her front door. There was no way he would allow her to ask him to leave. She didn't want him to go. Fucking him was utmost on her mind.

"You need to learn not to walk away from me." This time when he wrapped his arms around her, he grabbed her shirt, pulling it up to her waist.

"Oh." She didn't say anything else, her body crushing back against his as she turned to look up at him.

His goal had been reached. Triumph surged through him. Willing and of her own mind, Naomi would fuck him.

She moved easily when he held her waist and made her face him. He slid her shirt over her head, and she held her arms up, stretching her beautiful body as she slowly appeared before him naked.

He let her shirt drop to the floor.

"Damn. I couldn't have made you more perfect if I'd tried." He saw immediately that his words confused her but wouldn't allow her to dwell on them.

Cupping her breasts, feeling the soft fullness of them in his hands, he reached down and kissed her, stealing any words she might have said.

This wasn't a time for explanations. Right now all he wanted to do was explore her luscious body, enjoy the softness of her skin against his.

Kneading her breasts, pulling them toward him, she mewled into his mouth, the most perfect sound.

"I'm going to fuck your mouth, baby." He spoke in between kissing her, sucking on her lower lip while watching her eyes flutter open and shut.

With a mere thought, his boxers disappeared. He was out of practice, too accustomed to using his powers for everything. Capturing her without them had been a lot of work. And right now, the way she had him feeling, he had acted before thinking.

He thought of altering her thoughts, letting her believe she saw him undress. But he'd come this far. Although he'd lapsed for a moment, willing his clothing to disappear, free him of the restraints of the material that crushed his throbbing cock painfully, he wouldn't regress further.

"Your boxers," she began, glancing down him with a dazed expression.

She didn't fight him when he pressed on her shoulders, encouraging her to her knees. Going down on him, she eagerly took his cock into her mouth.

"By the gods," he cried out, the heat of her mouth saturating through him.

Steam filtered through his senses, everything around him disappearing except for the sensation of that hot little mouth sliding down his shaft.

"You are so good." He ran his hands through her hair, holding her head while those full lips slid over him, taking in all of him.

Just when she would have gagged, she sucked harder, gliding her tongue around his shaft, holding him in place while she slowly devoured him.

Her hair tangled around his fingers, the thick silky strands clinging to him while her head moved up and down over his cock. Tilting his head back, he let his eyes close, enjoying the best blowjob he'd had in a long time.

Blood pumped through him, leaving all parts of his body and flowing straight to his cock. He was light as a feather. Fighting the urge to float forward, bring his body over her so that he could better angle how deeply he penetrated her mouth, took his focus away from her mouth. If he weren't careful, he would explode right now. And he wouldn't let this end before he'd given her the pleasure that she craved.

And he could tell by the way she worked his cock that she wanted it badly.

"You want me to fuck you, don't you, baby?" He combed through her hair with his fingers.

She nodded, leaning back on her knees and allowing his cock to slide free from her mouth. Merco suddenly felt cold, too cold. He had to have the heat of her body wrapped around his cock again.

Her gaze swept over his body, taking in his physique. She lingered over certain parts of him, his chest, his cock, his legs, taking him into memory. When she glanced at his boxers, and he knew she wondered again how they had just fallen free of his body, he reached under her arms, lifting her.

"Turn around, darling," he instructed, distracting her thoughts and keeping them where he wanted them. All she need focus on was the fucking she was about to receive.

Naomi moaned when he turned her around and pressed down on her back until her hands flattened on her coffee table. She arched her back, spreading her legs slightly.

Merco simply stared at the incredible sight before him. Pressing into the softness of her ass, he spread her open, awestruck at the sight of those two tight-looking holes. She was perfectly shaven, the soft flesh surrounding her pussy and ass glistening with moisture.

"You are definitely a woman for a god." He hadn't meant to voice his thoughts.

But trying to think straight while his cock demanded to be buried deep inside her moist heat was proving harder and harder by the second.

His intention from the beginning had been to see if he could conquer this human without magic. And he'd managed quite nicely. He should be satisfied with his prize, enjoy it, and then be on his way.

He ran his thumbs over the smoothly shaven skin, her cum coating him while she jerked against his touch.

"Shit. Please." She turned her head, trying to look over her shoulder.

Her long hair fanned down her back, curling into tiny ringlets at the end. It draped over her like a robe, the soft red strands bringing out the creamy white of her skin. She could be a queen, her body so elegant, so perfect. The curve of her ass was so damned perfect. She was meant to be bent over, fucked good and hard and on a regular basis.

Damn it to hell. What were these thoughts about fucking her again? He hadn't even enjoyed her once yet and already he entertained visions of doing her on a regular basis. He didn't fuck any one woman on a regular basis. And no matter how hot this little redhead was, she wouldn't change his centuries-old way of life.

His cock was like a magnet against her cunt. He moved closer to her soaked hole. She seemed to draw him in, compel him forward with silent promises of giving him the best ride he'd ever had.

"I can't believe how fucking perfect you are." Again he spoke his thoughts out loud.

Could this little vixen have some kind of magic that he didn't know about? He knew that she didn't. He had simply indulged in fantasy women of his own creation for way too long, and the unknown of what Naomi might do next fed the fire within him until it burned out of control.

He pressed his cock against the slender slit. Fire consumed him, a volcano on the verge of erupting. Everything hardened inside him, his muscles clenching with such a severity that he couldn't breathe.

"Yes. Yes." She whipped her head from side to side, moving her ass against him in similar fashion. "Now. Damn it, now."

She lunged back against him, forcing his entrance before he could react. The breath he held shot out of his lungs so fast he growled in reaction. Never had anyone taken the upper hand in fucking him. Naomi had decided that she wanted him to fuck her, and by God if that wasn't what she would have. She was incredible. Absolutely fucking incredible.

Merco sank deep inside her hot moist walls. The moisture simmering around his shaft while her muscles clung to him, pulling him in further, brought his blood to a boil.

"You are so damn hot, so perfect and tight." He clenched his muscles, slowly pulling out of her so that he could enjoy the plunge again.

Her tight little cunt needed a good fucking.

"Merco." She cried out his name when he dove deep inside her again.

Gripping her ass he spread her apart, giving him the perfect view of his shaft, smeared with her thick white cream, sliding in and out of her taut pussy. He gritted his teeth, moving faster, needing to feel the friction burn into his cock. Pressure built inside him, his blood pounding through him. Every nerve ending inside him seemed way too sensitive. He was all too aware of her muscles constricting, quivering as he fucked her harder and harder.

"God. Oh, God. Yes." Her breathing was out of control. She bucked against him, her insides exploding with her orgasm.

He watched her tight little ass pucker while her cream soaked his cock and abdomen. Using his thumb, he smeared cum over her ass while he continued to impale her. That ass would be the perfect final treat. Watching his cum trickle out of that small hole would be his ultimate prize.

"That's it, baby. Come for me. That tight pussy of yours needed that, didn't it?" He slowed his momentum, allowing her time to catch her breath.

"Uh-huh." She let out a choked sigh, feeling the aftermath of her orgasm. "More. Please. I need more."

"I know you do." He stroked her back, feeling how moist her skin was. "And I'm going to give you more. We still have one more hole to satisfy. Do you want it there, baby?"

She stilled, her head turning while long wavy strands fell over her face. "I don't know," she said after a moment. "I've never had it there."

Merco began sliding his cock deep inside her pussy. Pulling out, he rammed her deep, hard, knowing with each thrust what would have to happen. And as he exploded, releasing his seed along the walls of her cunt, he wondered when his plan had changed.

"Next time, then." His uttered words sounded foreign to him. "Next time I'll fuck your ass."

Chapter Eight

Naomi didn't bother opening her eyes. Slowly coming to consciousness, the first thing she was aware of were the sore muscles running down her inner thighs. Getting out of bed might prove to be a challenge. And she wasn't sure she wanted to move yet anyway.

A slow throb between her legs started as she remembered everything that happened the night before. Never would she have dreamed she would have given in to Merco. But she had. And damn, what a wonderful time she'd had.

He had cuddled her into his arms, walked with her to her bedroom, pulled her covers back, and snuggled with her until they both fell asleep. She reached for him, wondering if he might want to go another round now.

"Merco?" she whispered, and then realized she was alone in her bed.

Naomi sat up quickly, ignoring the groaning muscles throughout her body as she threw back her covers. The floor was cold under her bare feet but she paid little attention, pushing her hair behind her shoulders as she padded into her living room and then to the kitchen.

She was alone in her apartment.

"Well, isn't this just lovely?" she said with disgust when she realized there was no note, no number, no indication at all that Merco had ever been here at all.

If it weren't for the sore muscles and the dampness between her legs she would wonder if she hadn't dreamed the whole thing. She stood in her kitchen doorway, staring into her living room, going over all the events of the evening before. He'd never mentioned anything about where he lived or worked. Hell, she knew nothing about the man.

"So you got what you wanted, Mr. Merco. And now you're gone." She pursed her lips in disgust and wrapped her arms around her waist, the cool air suddenly hitting her as she stood naked in her living room.

Not everything from the night before fell into place. Merco was a strange one. "He was just so damned good-looking," she confessed to herself, trying to justify why she'd allowed a complete stranger, who'd obviously broken into her apartment, to fuck her so thoroughly—so damned well.

And she couldn't help wondering about the man as she headed for a hot shower. There were things about him that just didn't add up. It still bugged her that he was able to get into her apartment without her hearing him enter.

He consumed her thoughts while she let the hot water pound her sore muscles. She prepared for work, not looking forward to her mundane job, and continued to replay the events from the night before. By the time she left her apartment, a smoldering urge to see him again, have another chance at figuring him out, and to fuck him again, had taken over. The chilly air outside didn't even faze her.

Amazingly, her shift flew by, and she headed out of the factory later that day, with co-workers coming and going around her with the shift-change.

"Naomi, wait up." Thena hurried around the group of people headed down the long, wide sidewalk toward the huge parking lot outside work. "Is everything okay?"

Naomi smiled at her friend.

Thena's pale brown eyes were full of concern, her brow lined and puckered as she scrutinized Naomi's face.

"Everything's fine. Why wouldn't it be?" Naomi sensed that her friend saw more than most.

A flutter started in her stomach, thoughts of Merco suddenly plaguing her with a vengeance. Not that he'd been far from her thoughts all day. But the slightest possibility existed that she might see him again. After all, he'd appeared out of nowhere before. Maybe he would do it again.

"You're strolling along in your own little world." Thena met her smile and her pretty eyes lit up. "What gives?"

"I might have met a guy." Naomi felt the warmth spread over her cheeks. It almost felt good against the cool late afternoon breeze.

"You might have met a guy?" Thena had walked with her to her car. She stood now, leaning against the side of it, studying Naomi. "What does that mean?"

"I met him the other night at the coven. His name is Merco." Naomi chewed her lower lip wondering how much to tell her friend.

A whistle blew from the factory, indicating the next shift. Thena glanced toward the building and then put her hand on Naomi's arm.

"I don't remember anyone there with that name," she said. "But I've got to go. I'm working second shift tonight, and I don't work tomorrow so maybe you will give me all the details then."

She gave Naomi a quick hug, and then trotted across the parking lot.

Naomi headed home, suddenly wanting someone to talk to about the strange man who had sauntered into her life, and then left without a clue. Bridget knew Merco. The thought hit Naomi with a sudden impact. She had warned Naomi to stay away from him, but her friend would support Naomi's decisions.

Not that she had a clue what decisions she'd made. Merco obviously held the ball in his court. He knew where she lived and how to reach her. She didn't know a damned thing about him. But she was about to find out.

She would take a cheerful attitude with Bridget. In all the years she had known her, the two of them having grown up in an orphanage together, there was one thing she had learned. Bridget could find the truth in the matter. She was a no-nonsense woman, beautiful and sharp, and with a drop-dead gorgeous man in her life. There was no harm in Naomi trying to learn more about Merco, and if she handled Bridget just right, she might learn something about the mystery man who'd fucked the tar out of her the night before.

And left her with promises of more.

"You're working late." Naomi let the large door close with a thud behind her.

Bridget sat at her workbench, her jeans and old sweatshirt doing nothing to conceal how pretty she was. Naomi had always envied her friend her natural grace, like a queen. She was nothing in comparison, her long thick strawberry blonde hair impossible to deal with, and her freckly white skin either looking sunburned or pale.

Bridget looked up at her, and then wiped her hands on a rag on the table. "Is everything okay?"

That was the second time she'd been asked that in the past hour. Maybe she was an open book, the words "sexual turmoil" printed across her forehead. She twisted the end of her braid, suddenly wondering if she shouldn't have just gone home and cuddled up in front of her TV.

But she was here. And the best way to deal with Bridget was to be straightforward. "I want you to tell me more about Merco," she said before she lost her nerve.

Bridget stood, walking toward her slowly, her gaze never leaving hers. For the briefest of moments she felt as if Bridget walked right through her, examining her every thought, every emotion.

"What do you want to know about him?" Bridget's tone was controlled, her presence almost unnerving.

Naomi forced herself to relax. After all, she was a grown woman. She and Bridget were friends. And she knew Bridget would respect any decision she made.

"He came to my place last night." In spite of the twisting knot of trepidation that began rippling through her gut, she pushed forward. "You said you knew him. So tell me about him."

"I said you should stay away from him." Bridget's tone was soft, concerned, even though she crossed her arms over her chest and gave Naomi a reprimanding look.

Naomi held her hand up. "I didn't come over here for you to mother me." And Bridget would do that to if she didn't stop her. "Now, you know I love you to death, but I can make my own decisions. Just give me the facts, ma'am."

Bridget sighed, turning from Naomi to walk over and stare down at her workbench. She combed her fingers through her hair, allowing the silence to grow in the large, airy workshop before letting out a soft sigh.

"What do you want to know?" Bridget gave her a side glance, chewing on her inner lip as if this conversation bothered her.

Naomi frowned. "Why do you want me to stay away from him?"

She hadn't meant for that to be her first question. She had hundreds of questions lined up, and that hadn't been one of them. But something about Bridget's expression, the worry line that interrupted the smooth skin on her forehead, grabbed her attention.

"There is a certain type of man..." Bridget searched for words, her gaze faltering before looking Naomi in the eye. "Merco isn't like most men you've met before. His sexual appetite is...how shall I say it...extreme."

A flush began deep inside Naomi's womb, spreading through her like a wildfire. Images of Merco's powerful chest, the thick ripple of black hair that curled over such well-defined muscles, stole her breath. She pictured those green eyes, hungry with a lust so intense the moisture spread between her legs just thinking about him.

"And you think I can't handle a man who likes to fuck?" Naomi itched to tell her friend how she'd taken Merco on the night before.

But that would accomplish nothing. Not to mention, she wasn't sure Bridget would understand why she had submitted to a man who had broken into her apartment, and now wondered how she could learn more about him. She didn't understand her heated curiosity.

Bridget shook her head, looking like she tried to rid herself of unpleasant thoughts. "You don't understand. I've known Merco a long time. He is a very good friend of Braze." She looked at Naomi, licking her lips, once again appearing that she searched for the right words. "Merco indulges in a sexual lifestyle that I don't think you've ever experienced."

Naomi's heart began pounding a little too fast. Suddenly her mouth went dry. "A sexual lifestyle?"

Bridget nodded. "Naomi. You could have any man you wanted. Just look at you. You are so pretty and independent. Any man would enjoy being with you. Merco isn't for you. He is way too sexually promiscuous."

Naomi had a sudden thought of Merco tying her up, using sex toys to make her explode into sexual bliss. Her breath caught in her throat, the pounding of her heart moving between her legs.

"No. It's not like you think." Bridget pursed her lips into a thin line. "He likes to make his women perform, Naomi. Do you understand? He enjoys watching, sharing, orgies."

Bridget's words hit Naomi hard. She wanted nothing to do with a player, with someone who had such little respect for their body in a world full of terrible diseases. She wouldn't be a man's slave, to be used sexually for his own warped amusement, with no thoughts of her own pleasure. And her heart sank as she left Bridget's workshop and headed home.

"Will you stop by the apartment after a bit?" Bridget called after her. "I should be home soon."

Naomi opened her car door, nodding and waving. "Maybe I will," she hollered. Maybe it would be best to hang out with her friends, instead of wallowing in misery alone in her own apartment.

And maybe Merco would come to her again if she were to stay home alone.

But if he didn't…she ran the chance of falling asleep early and risking her nightmares. Just the thought of the nasty demon that tormented her sleep gave her the shivers. She couldn't get her car heater to warm up fast enough.

Several hours later, the cold night air seemed to wrap around her in her apartment. Naomi wrapped up in an afghan on her couch, deciding to call Bridget instead of going over there. But since there was no answer, she assumed her friend had something come up.

"Maybe their apartment is too cold to hang out in, too," she mused, standing up to check her thermostat.

It showed the apartment should be a balmy eighty degrees, yet she swore she could see her breath. Her nipples were so hard they hurt under her sweatshirt, and it was all she could do to keep her teeth from chattering.

If Merco showed up, she bet he would keep her warm.

Cuddling under her blanket and staring at the show on TV that she was paying absolutely no attention to, she imagined Merco strolling through her door. So tall and dark, well-built and confident, it wouldn't take much to convince her that he was a product of her imagination. And if Bridget hadn't acknowledged knowing him, she might have wondered if she hadn't simply conjured him up.

Something about his appearing out of nowhere, refusing to tell her how he'd entered her apartment, gave him a dangerous air. That excited her even more. He didn't take no for an answer, yet demanded that she tell him she wanted him.

Her pussy began throbbing, and she reached inside her blanket, running her hand under the elastic of her sweatpants. The warmth from her pussy wrapped around her cold fingers. And when she touched herself, she sucked in a breath. Hot moisture wrapped around her chilled fingers.

"Oh, damn," she murmured, separating the smooth flesh between her legs and probing deeper.

If these were Merco's fingers, touching her, spreading her, moving deep inside her, she would be begging him to fuck her. Her small hand couldn't reach where she knew he could reach, couldn't soothe the ache that she knew he could appease.

She exhaled, her breath clouding in front of her face as the room seemed to grow even colder. It wasn't right to fantasize about Merco. If what Bridget said was true, she should force the man out of her thoughts, refuse to give him the time of day. Even if the only time she was giving him was in her imagination.

"That's right, my precious slut, you shouldn't be thinking about that useless god. His powers won't help you now." The menacing voice that haunted her dreams and turned them into nightmares sounded like it came from right next to her.

"Shit!" Naomi screamed, almost falling off the couch as she yanked her hand out of her soaked pussy and then struggled with the blanket that tangled around her.

She looked frantically around her apartment, seeing no one. It made no sense. That was the hissing sound of the demon, and she hadn't been asleep.

And what did he mean about useless god? Or powers? Naomi shoved the blanket away, shaking furiously but no longer caring that she was cold. Something was seriously wrong here.

"He won't come to you again, you slut." The voice came from right behind her.

Naomi spun around, making herself dizzy. Again no one was there.

"You belong to me. To me!" He shouted the words at her, this time his voice seeming to come from all around her.

Naomi tried to lick her dry lips, but her tongue was just as parched. Shaking, she looked around her wide-eyed, too terrified to organize her thoughts.

"Where are you?" she asked, knowing she really didn't want to know. "Leave me alone."

She sounded pathetic even to herself.

Silence loomed around her. Her heart pounded in her chest as she glanced at the reporter, chatting cheerfully on the TV about something. She continued a visual survey of her living room. Tangling her fingers in her braided hair she tried to regain control of her wits.

Someone touched her, and she spun around, or tried to. A bony grip held her in place while long groping fingers ripped at her breasts.

"No!" she screamed, lunging forward away from the demon.

He let go of her and she toppled to the floor, her hands and knees burning instantly when she scraped them along her carpet.

"Get out of here and leave me alone." She fell backwards, scurrying crablike with her rear end dragging on the floor toward the door of her apartment.

"There is nowhere that you can run and escape me." His voice seemed inches from her face, so close that she could smell the foul breath that she knew all too well from her nightmares. "There is no one you can run to, either. No one would believe you. They would shake their head and label you a fool. Do you understand? You are mine." His words sliced through her, sending her into a panic.

"Stop it," she cried out. "Please. Why are you doing this to me?"

The door behind her moved and she jumped, terror making it hard to think straight.

"Naomi." Bridget's concerned voice came from the other side of the door. Then a bit louder, more urgent, her friend called out again. "Naomi. Let me in."

Naomi scooted away from the door, surprised to see it open easily. In the next instant, her friend had her wrapped in her arms, holding her securely while she began soothing tones.

"It's okay. We're here now. You're going to be okay."

"Mention anything about me, you little slut, and I will make your nightmares look like child's play." The demon's voice whispered brutally through her.

Naomi shivered, icy fingers creeping down her spine giving her goose bumps. She clung to Bridget without realizing what she did.

"She's terrified and I can't tell why," she heard Bridget say to Braze who stood over her.

Chapter Nine

Ten minutes later, Naomi sat on her couch with a doubtful Bridget and Braze looking down at her.

"I'm fine. Really I am." She was anything but fine, but as much as she hated to admit it, the demon was right. There was no way they would believe her if she told them the truth.

Bridget turned, looking up at Braze and she watched while the two stared at each other, seeming to speak to each other without talking. She found her tummy twisting, envying them the bond that they shared. Maybe someday, if she were lucky, she would have a relationship like that.

A soft tapping on her door made her jump. Both Bridget and Braze turned to look at her closed door, although neither of them moved. Bridget let out a sigh when Naomi got up to answer it. She realized her legs were shaking when she pulled the door open.

Merco stood on the other side of the door, in the hallway, looking larger than life, and very concerned.

Which, of course, was her imagination. The man had no idea what she had just been through.

He wore blue jeans that looked well-worn and molded against his long muscular legs. No man ever made a simple T-shirt look so delicious. The material stretched over his chest, his muscular arms bulging where the shirt sleeves ended. Her mouth was suddenly no longer dry. Instead, she found she was on the verge of drooling.

"You need me." The calm assurance in his tone made his statement almost sound dangerous.

She couldn't have spoken if she wanted. Moving to the side, she held the door open allowing him into her living room. For the life of her she wished she were in anything other than her old faded sweatshirt and sweatpants. She had to look like shit. And he—he looked like perfection.

Tall and so well-built, he made a Greek god look like a schoolboy. Something in his stance, in the expression on his face, gave her the impression he would pounce at the first sign of danger, taking on any threat without hesitation. If he weren't making her so damned wet between her thighs at that very moment, she would consider him terrifying.

"What are you doing here, Merco?" Bridget's tone was calm, yet reprimanding.

Merco didn't take his gaze off of Naomi. "I stopped in at your place, and no one was home."

"Liar," Bridget mumbled and Braze ran his hand down the back of her head, giving her hair a slight tug.

He looked up at Merco with a relaxed smile. Naomi got the impression that they all knew each other very well.

"How are you doing, old friend?" Braze asked, reaching out with his free hand to shake Merco's hand.

"Merco, why don't you wait for us down at our apartment?" Bridget seemed anxious to get him out of Naomi's apartment.

Merco looked down at Naomi. "I'm not going anywhere without her."

His expression was relaxed, not a single crease in his forehead, no worry lines around his mouth. Those sexy green eyes probed deep inside her, pulling at emotions that were already too frazzled to get organized. Something changed in his expression while he stared at her. A muscle twitching next to his mouth was her only clue.

She forced herself to blink, to break the spell he seemed to put her under the second she'd opened her door. Her breath suddenly came too fast, her mouth too dry to speak. Just being near this man seemed to throw her entire insides off balance. The moisture between her legs grew, a slow throbbing distracting her, while memories of what he was capable of doing to her body suddenly took over her rational thought.

"Merco..." Bridget began.

But Braze stopped her with a touch, placing his hand on her shoulder. "Merco won't do anything to hurt her."

Bridget made a snorting sound. Naomi looked at her, and then slowly looked at the two men. All of them watched her, as if they expected something from her. She had no idea what to say. Hell, yes, she wanted Merco to stay. There was no way she could be alone in her apartment.

"Make them go away." The hissing threat in her head from the nasty creature made her duck. "Get rid of all of them right now or I swear you'll regret it."

She didn't mean to react so visibly to the demon. But never had he spoken to her when others had been around. Up until now, he'd only harassed her while she slept. A chill wrapped around her and she fought to cover up her unexpected movement by walking away from all three of them.

"What just happened?" she heard Merco ask.

She turned around, ready to apologize for her sudden movement. It took everything she had not to walk into that powerful chest of his, seek out his warmth, his security. She didn't know why. But for some reason she was sure the demon wouldn't harass her if she were with Merco.

"Naomi." Bridget reached for her, placing her slender hand on Naomi's shoulder.

"I can't pick anything up other than she is terrified." Braze said that, his voice full of concern.

"Naomi. Come here." Merco also approached her.

"No, Merco." Bridget sounded stern.

Naomi frowned, catching the worried expressions on all of their faces.

"Bridget, she is a grown woman. You can't play mother hen to all of them." Merco looked like he would pat Bridget on the head.

Bridget placed her fists on her hips. "Why this one? If you are just playing around, go mess with another lady's head."

"Quit it. Both of you." She couldn't handle her best friend and Merco bickering like this. "I decide who messes with my head."

The way Bridget looked at her made her realize how ridiculous her words had just sounded. She held the same stern expression when she turned her attention to Merco.

"And I won't have any man messing with my head," she added quickly, feeling the heat flush through her cheeks when he cocked an eyebrow at her.

"That's it. Make them leave." The demon spoke louder in her thoughts. "I'm the only one who shall be inside you. I will torture that luscious body of yours, enjoying every inch of you until you scream and beg to do whatever I wish. That cunt of yours will be mine to devour."

"Stop it," she screamed, covering her face with her hands, wishing she could scratch the demon out of her head. She wanted to yell out that she would keep her friends here forever if he didn't quit taunting her.

"Don't even dare to threaten me. Not even in your thoughts." A piercing pain drove through her, like a spear had pierced her at the tip of her head and drove its fierce point clear through her, impaling her.

Naomi gasped, sucking in a staggered breath, doing her best not to stagger from the outrageous infliction. In the next instant it was gone, dissipating as if it had never been there.

"She isn't talking to us," Braze said.

"You're right. But why can't we hear it, too?" Merco asked.

"She needs protection," Bridget said, and then placed her warm hands on Naomi's arms. "Naomi, you're staying with us until we figure out what is wrong."

"I'll protect her." Merco reached for her.

His hands were like a magnet, calling her body to him as he opened to her, willing her to come to him. She took a step toward him.

Scared to breathe, not sure what this creature in her head was capable of, all she knew was that he was much more than a terrible nightmare.

"Naomi." Bridget stepped in front of Merco, cupping Naomi's face with her hands. "Tell me what is going on. Do you see someone else here besides us?"

"That's crazy." Naomi couldn't help a small laugh that bordered on sounding hysterical. Her heart raced painfully in her chest and she looked over Bridget's shoulder at Merco. "There isn't anyone here besides us."

"Something upset you when you called me to you last night," Merco offered, his green eyes searching hers, filling her chilled body with warmth as she drowned in his gaze.

Bridget's expression hardened at his words. She let go of Naomi, sighing. Bridget's green eyes pierced through her, while she ran her slender fingers through her long hair.

"Tell me what is bothering you," she said softly, her tone comforting, reassuring that they were still good friends.

Bone-like fingers suddenly pressed against the shaven skin between Naomi's legs. Underneath her sweatpants, a hand crawled over her pussy. Probing and pushing her tender folds apart, the knobby fingers thrust inside her, a silent warning of what she would endure if she shared her nightmare with her friends.

Tears welled in her eyes before she could stop them. She fisted her hands at her side, clamping her teeth together, forcing her mind to accept that the hand wasn't really there. No one was trying to finger-fuck her. She didn't understand the mind games this terrible demon played with her. But he wouldn't win.

Cold sweat broke out over her body, terror riveting through her while she fought not to let her teeth chatter. Her heart raced in her chest, the urge to run from the apartment, run from all of them, run until this beast left her alone, consuming her.

But that would be ridiculous. She couldn't run from a thought. From a nightmare that now haunted her while she was awake.

Taking a step backwards from all of them, the back of her legs hit against the coffee table. "I can't tell you. I mean, there is nothing to tell."

They were all looking at her like she was crazy. And the confused expression on Merco's face was worst of all. His dark skin made his thick brown hair appear almost shiny. Waving around his face, accentuating his strong features, he was a god. The sexiest man she'd ever laid eyes on. And here he was, standing in her living room giving her a pitiful look.

She would die of embarrassment and humiliation before this night was over.

"Come with me," he said, his words leaving no room for discussion.

Naomi worked to swallow. He held his hand out to her and her surroundings seemed to disappear.

"No!" the demon creature screamed in her head. "Stay away from him. He will torture you worse than even I can."

She didn't believe him. Nothing could be more torturous than the hideous demon.

Merco smiled as if he heard her thoughts, felt her dilemma, and wished to reassure her. That smile did a number on her insides. In spite of her fear, of her near panic that the creature would destroy her sanity right there in her own living room in front of the few friends she had, that smile made her tummy do a flip-flop.

He might be dangerous, preoccupied with an obsession for sex that she couldn't comprehend but her body screamed for another chance to be with him.

Glancing at Bridget, she saw her friend's concern. Braze had pulled Bridget into his arms, watching Naomi over her head.

Naomi took a step toward Merco and the pain hit her again, driving through her skull, rupturing every cell inside her. She doubled over, unable to conceal her reaction to what was happening to her.

"Where did you cast the demon leader?" Merco sounded fierce as he gave Bridget a hard look.

His strong hands suddenly were on Naomi, holding her, lifting her against his chest.

"Damn it all to Hedel," Bridget swore. "There is no way he could have…"

Her words broke off. Merco held her now, his powerful grip pinning her to him. Her body throbbed, pulsated, the pain subsiding while torturous need enveloped her. She stared at Bridget, preoccupied at the same time with Merco's body touching her practically everywhere.

"What demon?" She was almost scared to ask.

Chapter Ten

Merco would not manipulate her in any way. He'd made a vow—a promise to himself. And damn it to all the hells if he would break it now.

Naomi was in trouble. It didn't take power to figure that one out. And he had no regrets bringing her home with him when she'd collapsed.

Watching her now, stretched across his bed, her long legs twisted in his covers, the slow steady, rise and fall of her tummy, while her breasts remained full, perky, her nipples erect, she looked more beautiful the longer he stared.

Her long red hair twisted into ringlets and fanned around her, looking radiant against his white silk sheets. One of her arms stretched to the edge of the bed while her other hand curled into a fist next to her cheek. Her eyelashes fluttered, a dream rushing through her. She looked so peaceful yet he could tell her mind raced through the actions of some event in her sleep.

"What plagues you, beautiful?" he whispered, willing himself inside her mind as he studied her.

Something blocked him, though, and it wasn't Naomi. She was being tormented, influenced by someone's magic, and that didn't sit well with him. Not at all.

He moved to the side of the bed, leaning forward enough to run his finger along her leg. She didn't stir, her dream didn't hesitate. Whoever or whatever had a hold on her wasn't concerned with his presence. That irritated him even further.

Nothing that he was aware of in this galaxy held more power than the gods—the elders of Hedel. They were the known strength that had seeded the universe. They controlled everything. Yet somehow, something had lodged its way inside Naomi, and didn't give a rat's ass that he stood there frowning down at it.

"Get out of her now," he hissed, leaning over her sleeping body, watching her eyelids flutter while her eyes darted back and forth under the fragile skin.

Naomi gasped in her sleep, her full lips parting, that sensual mouth curving as if she would utter a word. Yet she said nothing.

Something dark and forbidding shuddered through Merco. He watched her, not moving, while his insides hardened, a silent predatory instinct overwhelming him. Stalk and destroy whatever plagued her.

He was so close to her, looking down over her, and he had even spoken out loud. She should stir, come out of her sleep, react to his presence somehow. Yet she slumbered, not stirring. This was terribly wrong.

Pulling her out of her dream would be nothing. With a blink of an eye he could wake her, make her want him, fuck her until she couldn't come anymore. That would be effortless, and his cock hardened at the thought.

"No," he told himself, refusing to use his powers to influence her.

He had told himself when he first sought her out that he would seduce her without powers. Every muscle inside of him hardened, the realization that possibly he wanted more than a seduction.

The need to protect her couldn't be denied. And it would be so easy to do with his powers. But the fact that she slept soundly, that he couldn't hear or see her dream, only told him that she wasn't responding to him.

"Damn it." He stood, running his fingers through his hair, the sight of her plump breasts making his mouth water.

Never had he wanted a woman more. He moved toward the bedroom door, ignoring his plush surroundings, her presence distracting him more than he cared to admit. Need burned through him, a pressure that he wasn't accustomed to ignoring growing more and more uncomfortable by the moment.

When was the last time he'd walked away from a naked woman on his bed? Had he ever refrained from fucking a woman if he was inclined to do so?

Something about Naomi had crept through his system, made him want to see the bargain through he'd made with himself. But right now she didn't need to be seduced. She needed to be protected, taken care of, and he had a burning need to do just that.

And that didn't sit well with him. Turning, he stared once again at her beautiful body, now appearing more relaxed than she had a minute before. She rolled to the side, the covers moving with her, leaving her smooth round ass exposed and so tempting.

His fingers itched to touch that soft curve, to feel the silky texture of her skin.

"Naomi." He spoke her name out of need more than wishing to wake her.

His body screamed to be one with her, feel the heat from being buried deep inside her. He took a step closer to the bed, and then made himself stop, balling his hands into fists at his side. Grinding his teeth, feeling the ache grow as his cock throbbed in his jeans, he closed his eyes for a moment. Which didn't do a damn bit of good. Her image was branded in his thoughts, her fresh scent filled his nostrils, taking over as if it were her casting the spell.

"You are nothing more than a mortal," he whispered through clenched teeth, willing himself to believe that she should adore him, sing his praises, worship him.

Just as her kind had done for centuries.

Shaking his head, he turned again. Naomi wasn't just another mortal. She was a woman, simple and unique. And for some reason she had gotten under his skin and it appeared she planned to stay there for a while.

"And who said humans couldn't cast spells." He made himself leave his room, disgusted with his thoughts that she should think him anymore than what he was.

A horny immortal who had used women for way too many centuries.

"Merco." The woman's voice calling him confused him for the briefest of seconds.

Momentarily, he allowed his mind to think that Naomi called for him. He had just shut his bedroom door and he turned to stare at it.

"There you are." Bridget spoke from the top of the stairs, concern on her face as she stared down the hallway at him.

Merco turned, staring at her, knowing before asking why she was here.

"Hurt her and I swear I will kick your ass." She thought her words instead of speaking them.

Merco didn't smile, knowing she meant it. He'd known Bridget since her youth, had watched over the centuries as her powers had grown. She'd had a run-in with the leader of the demons, and had lost her identity for a handful of centuries. But today, just a year or so since she had regained knowledge of who she was, she had complete control of her powers. He didn't doubt she would be a fair match, and possibly capable of doing him harm if she caught him off-guard.

Relaxing, he floated over the banister, and Bridget followed him down the stairs. Her frustration and anger filled the air around them. Merco wasn't daunted by it. Bridget could play the protective friend all she wanted. He knew damn good and well he hadn't done anything wrong, and if anything, he had done the right thing in bringing Naomi here when she collapsed. There was no way in hell he would leave her there in that apartment. Not until he figured out what had her acting the way she did. And he didn't like the possibilities.

"Is she here?" Braze knew the answer to that.

Merco simply stared at him. His usually jovial friend gave him a hard stare. It didn't intimidate him in the least. He landed in the living room and walked over to the bar. Holding out his hands he made a tray appear with three tall glasses, clinking with ice cubes. All of them could use a drink.

"Something is terribly wrong here." He turned to face both of them, holding out the tray.

Bridget hesitated a moment and then accepted the drink, her long brown locks flowing over her shoulder and down her front. She was a beautiful woman, intelligent and sexy. At the moment her brow wrinkled, though, her short fingers, with her fingernails clipped short, brushing through her hair. The absent movement showed how distracted she was, how upsetting all of this was to her. That explained his friend's serious look.

"No shit." Braze took a large gulp of his drink, glanced down at it, and changed it to a dark golden fluid. He then took another drink. "How many times have you fucked her so far?"

Merco raised an eyebrow, an instant image of Naomi lying naked on his bed, her long red hair streaming down her creamy skin, consuming his thoughts.

"Just once." He knew why they asked, fucking could strengthen powers. "She's mortal, though."

"But what if she is possessed?" Bridget asked, her worry turning to anger. "Merco. Naomi means a lot to me. She may just be another play toy to you, but you are fucking my dear friend."

He almost said she was more than a play toy. A warmth spread through him, an emotion he couldn't identify. He cared about her. There was something wrong and she needed his protection. His insides burned with the thought that anyone would abuse her, possess her against her will. Granted he didn't know her well, but he wouldn't walk away and leave her suffering.

"You don't give me much credit," he told her, relaxing his features, trying to get his insides to calm down, too.

"That's because I know you so well." Bridget floated several feet above the ground, crossing her legs, and sitting comfortably in her faded jeans and T-shirt while she levitated. "I don't understand why we can't figure out what is bothering Naomi, though," she mused, staring down at her glass.

"She shows all the signs of being possessed." Braze paced over to the windows that overlooked Merco's well manicured yard.

Merco moved to his couch, reclining and stretching his legs out in front of him underneath his glass coffee table. He finished off his drink and then let go of the glass. It disappeared and another appeared, this time with water. He didn't feel like getting drunk. Naomi upstairs in his bedroom distracted him too much. Going up there to her right now wasn't an option. But damn it to hell if he didn't want to be with her.

"If she were possessed, I would have seen the demon inside her." And the motherfucker would have died a torturous death. "Besides, the demons are real scarce these days since Bridget destroyed their leader."

"You care about her," Bridget almost whispered. "I never thought I would see such compassion in you, Merco. What is this?"

Both of them studied him. He didn't have to look up to know that.

Compassion…caring…he did care for Naomi. What happened to her did matter to him. There was no ignoring the warmth that flushed through him every time he thought about her.

"I know the difference between a human woman, and a woman of my own creation." He didn't want to justify thoughts that he wasn't ready to acknowledge on his own. But he knew Bridget. She wouldn't let it rest until he satisfied her curiosity. "I'm not in love with her. But I don't want to see her hurt, either. And I will protect her if needed."

"Leave him alone, Bridget." Braze finally came to his defense. Morning sunlight streamed through the glass behind him when he walked toward the center of the room toward her. "We all know there is a problem here. The question is, what is bothering Naomi? And why can't we readily detect it in her thoughts?"

Merco was no expert on demons. He usually managed to avoid the nasty creatures. And they sure as hell never sought him out.

"Somehow it's managed to mask itself from us." Bridget straightened her legs until her feet touched the ground.

Grabbing her hair from behind her neck, she twisted it, making him think of what it would be like to take Naomi's hair like that, pull her head back, make her back arch, while he drove his cock deep inside her.

She was just up the stairs, sleeping on his bed. The urge to leave his body, float up the stairs and plant kisses down her until she cooed herself awake made his cock soar to life in his jeans.

Naomi's sensuality amazed him. He had brought her desires to life without powers, without coercing her, and she had fucked him better than any of his own creations ever had. She was a gift, and one he wasn't going to readily give up.

There had to be a way to rid her of whatever plagued her.

"No demon can stand on the altar at Hedel," he mused, thinking out loud.

"You want to take her into the coven?" Braze asked, tossing his glass into the air and watching as it vanished. He grinned at Bridget, taking a step toward her. "They thought you a mere member of the village when you first approached the coven."

She swatted at him, although her expression was playful. "And you know as well as I do that I wasn't. Naomi is a mortal. She has no powers. I would know by now if she did."

She had the power to consume his thoughts.

Something stirred. Although not visible, he felt the stirring, knew the instant she awoke. Putting his feet on his coffee table, he crossed one leg over the other and relaxed further, staring up at the ceiling.

Merco saw through the plaster, through the beams in the ceiling. Naomi sat up on the bed. Her confusion was mixed from grogginess. But curiosity was her strongest emotion.

He ached for her. With every fiber in his body he wanted to be by her side right now, pulling her into his arms, allowing her to awake slowly while he held her.

"She's awake," Bridget said unnecessarily.

They all sensed it.

"We need to talk this out," Braze said, and waved a hand in the air. "She'll sleep until we are done."

Merco didn't like how Naomi suddenly collapsed on the bed, a victim to Braze's simple spell to make her fall back asleep.

"No." He reversed the spell instantly, allowing her to wake up again. "There will be no magic placed on her."

He met the curious gazes of his friends. "I won't have it," he added.

"How interesting." Bridget gave him a long, hard look. She guessed he was becoming too involved with

Naomi, and her emotions were clear. She didn't like it. "Do you plan to tell her who you really are?"

"No." He decided he needed another drink. Holding out his hand, a glass appeared. "I don't want her thoughts altered. Her decisions will be her own."

Bridget glanced at Braze. He took her hand and pulled her to him, then looked over his shoulder at Merco.

"I believe you will care for her. We will leave you with her, then. But see here, my friend, if you do her wrong, you will have both of us to answer to." Braze meant it, too. He would defend Naomi's honor because she was Bridget's friend.

Naomi had some good friends.

Merco nodded, knowing beyond a doubt that Naomi was safest with him. Whatever troubled her, he would find out. And he would rid her of it.

"You better treat her right." Bridget wagged a finger at him, and then she and Braze disappeared.

Chapter Eleven

Naomi froze on the stairs. Her heart thudded against her ribs, and for a second she thought she might plunge forward, losing her balance and falling to the floor below.

She didn't have a clue where in the hell she was, or how'd she gotten there. This luxurious palace, this elegant manor, this…this mansion…was unlike anywhere she'd ever been before. And she was pretty sure she wasn't dreaming.

And then descending the stairs, hearing the familiar voices below, the first person she'd seen was Merco.

The man took her breath away. Leaning back on a beautiful white couch with his dark skin contrasting against it, his muscular arms spread over the back of it, and his long thick legs relaxed lazily on the coffee table, he looked very much at home. She couldn't steal her gaze away. Butterflies had pranced through her tummy, fluttering around without a care while she struggled to breathe normally. There couldn't possibly be better eye candy on the entire planet.

Bridget and Braze had their backs to her, and spoke quietly to him. They partially blocked her view, but she paid them little attention.

That was until they disappeared.

Fucking disappeared. As if they'd never been there.

She couldn't move—couldn't think. How could they just disappear?

One minute they had been there, standing next to each other, talking to Merco. The next they minute they vanished, disappeared into thin air.

Reality had ceased to exist for her. That had to be it. She had gone completely insane.

Without thinking—hell she couldn't fathom a thought at that moment had she tried—Naomi bolted down the stairs, running in the opposite direction of Merco.

She'd wanted to run to him, into those powerful arms. Leaning against that strong body, letting him hold her and assure her that her mind had just played tricks on her sounded real damned good. The way his gaze had shifted, his eyes moving while his body remained relaxed until he focused on her, made her think twice. As soon as Bridget and Braze vanished, he'd looked at her with those green eyes that seemed to glow, penetrate right through her. And she'd panicked.

He'd called out her name. Or at least she thought he had. A ringing started in her head, making it impossible for her to focus on anything she heard around her. Merco hadn't seemed a bit surprised that they vanished.

What the fuck was going on?

Fear had gripped her, taking over her rational thought. She had found a door, run across thick well-groomed grass, and hit a sidewalk, taking it at racing speed, before it dawned on her to look around to see where she was.

"Don't slow down now, bitch," the demon hissed in her head, causing her brain to throb painfully while he spat out his words. "Run with the speed I will grace you with. Only I will protect you from those gods. Run. Run!"

Naomi had found her clothes when she woke up in the strange bed, but hadn't given a thought to her shoes. She glanced down at her bare feet and then at her surroundings. She was in one of the wealthiest areas of Kansas City known as Westboro—very much out of her element. Johnson County's Westboro area housed some of the wealthiest families in the nation. Exquisite mansions rested behind tall iron gates and large well-kept yards. If she was lucky, a gardener would see her.

But did she want the police called? What would she tell them?

The voice in my head won't leave me alone. And a man I'm in lust with might not be human. Shit. She wasn't sure if her health plan covered being institutionalized.

She picked up her pace, ignoring the taunting the demon gave her as she hurried to get out of the exclusive neighborhood. Her legs hurt from walking the steep hills before she reached an intersection, one of the wealthier shopping areas spread out in front of her known as The Plaza. This wasn't a part of town she frequented on a regular basis—barefoot, carless, and with no purse or identification on her—this was not good.

Somehow she needed to find a phone. An ornate clock on one of the tall buildings ahead told her she had ten minutes to get to work. All she needed now was to fuck up her job.

"Run, bitch. They will catch you. Use you. Listen to me, you fucking bitch, and run!" The hissing of the demon vibrated against her skull.

Her head pounded as she mentally told it to shut up and leave her alone. Doing her best to ignore the pain that rushed through her body as punishment for not paying heed to the demon, she walked to a convenience store. The street was lined with recently planted trees all the same size, and thick grass covered with morning dew that instantly made her feet cold and wet. She hurried, praying the person working would have mercy and allow her to use the phone.

Although he gave her an odd look, the college kid behind the counter handed her the cordless, and she quickly called in sick to work. Then hanging up, she dialed another number quickly before the employee protested that she made more than one call.

"Thena." She gave silent thanks that her friend answered her cell phone on the first ring, although she sounded groggy since her shift was almost over. "I need a favor…a big favor."

Naomi hated doing this. Thena had worked all night and would be ready to go home and crash. Normally she would call Bridget if she were in a bind. Her head pounded, her thoughts a mixture of panic and confusion while she hid in the convenience store bathroom, leaning her head against the stall while she waited out the ten minutes her friend told her it would take before she could pick her up.

"Do you think you can hide from him in here?" the demon laughed as he ridiculed her. "You stupid cunt. They can find you anywhere. You will pay me back dearly for concealing you. But know now, all he wants is that sweet pussy of yours. And it is mine. Is that clear? Mine!"

She gripped her head, tangling her fingers in her hair. "Leave me alone," she whispered angrily, praying she could figure out a way to cast him out of her head. "I'm not yours. I will never be yours."

It felt like someone had just punched her in the gut, and she doubled over, almost tripping over the toilet behind her in the small stall.

"Fuck you. Nothing you do to me will make me agree that I belong to you. You might as well give up now." She staggered out of the stall, splashing water on her face while she fought the pain that he ripped through her body.

Somehow she had to manage herself in public. Thena would be there soon and she needed to wait for her outside.

A small part of her wished Merco would be out there, too, looking for her. He confused her, the way he had looked at her after Bridget and Braze disappeared. He hadn't been surprised, not at all. His intent stare was branded in her mind, a look that had demanded she just accept what had happened, and not question it.

And seeing his face in her mind, the way he'd bored through her, his stare controlled, predatory, had her pussy throbbing. The overwhelming desire to turn and march right up that hill toward that mansion of his, spread through her like wild fire. She burned with a need for him, craved his hands on her, controlling her, seducing her.

Who was he? He had appeared in her locked apartment, coming to her when she couldn't sleep. Although she should have kicked him out, called the police, somehow he had seduced her, made her want him. And damn it to hell if she didn't want him again right now.

The morning sun shone down on her, the neighborhood relatively quiet since the workday had already begun. Glancing up the hill where one mansion after another spread out over rolling hills and beautiful lawns, she wondered what kind of person Merco was. What did he do for a living? Who the hell was he?

One didn't just idly run into a person who lived in one of those estates. That was old money, the elite and prestigious. And to have met him at a coven, a meeting of witches of all places. Did he practice witchcraft?

Naomi shook her head, her thoughts still not working properly. No witch she'd ever met could make people disappear—vanish into thin air.

"Naomi. Are you okay?" Thena had pulled up in front of her and rolled down the passenger window.

"Thank you for picking me up." Naomi collapsed into the passenger seat, closing the door next to her. She didn't answer her friend's question, though.

Hell, no, she wasn't okay. And Thena deserved an explanation. Her concerned look as her gaze swept over Naomi's appearance told her that she wouldn't press for answers. That was a damned good thing. Because Naomi wasn't sure where to begin. But she needed help—she needed a lot of help.

A tall, dark, rather powerful-looking stranger had invaded her life. She wanted him, yet she'd just run from him. Something about him wasn't right and she just couldn't put her finger on it. But damn it to hell if thinking about him didn't make her insides flutter, her juices begin to flow. She'd been in his bed, that overly large bed with the silk sheets. His scent had been everywhere, her insides melting while she consumed his aura, remembered how he'd made her explode over and over again the night he'd appeared out of nowhere and seduced her. And part of her wished she had never gotten up, never gone down those stairs, never seen Bridget and Braze disappear.

"Something terrible has happened," Thena was saying. "I can sense it."

Her friend reached over and squeezed her hand. They were on the interstate now, the exits passing by as they drove to the part of Kansas City where Thena lived.

"Remember the man I told you about…the one I met at the coven?" Naomi began, and then told Thena how he'd come to her.

She didn't mention how he'd infuriated her that night, but at the moment that seemed a trivial fact.

"Damn. He sounds sexy as hell." Thena's words were lighthearted but when Naomi looked over at her she saw the concern on her face.

"He is sexy as hell," she murmured, looking down at her lap, wondering if she'd done the right thing by running from him.

The demon seemed to have left her alone for now, and her head was clear to dwell on Merco. She hesitated in trusting him. She had run from him. But why did she ache all over to be with him?

Somehow she needed to clear her head, really clear her head. It would be the only way she could focus on what was happening around her, and in her mind.

"You aren't going to believe me," Naomi began, shaking her head. She didn't believe most of this herself. "But I really need to talk, need someone else to see what I'm seeing and tell me I'm not crazy."

"You'd be surprised what I might believe." Thena chuckled, a refreshing sound. Her friend's brown eyes lit up with interest. "Tell me everything. It will make you feel better."

They merged through the midmorning traffic and Thena signaled for her exit. Entering into a quiet neighborhood, clean yet simple houses appeared on either side of them, such a different atmosphere from where they'd been just ten minutes ago.

It took a few minutes to get to Thena's home and she hurried around the house, making sure Naomi was comfortable before they settled down at a small square table in Thena's kitchen. Hot water simmered for tea, and different scents rose lazily in the air from the several candles Thena lit. She brought an old wooden bowl to the table, a mixture of herbs crushed at the bottom of it. Running her long thin fingers through the herbs, she stirred them up, whispering words to the gods to soothe their minds, allow their conversation to be blessed.

Naomi took a long breath and forced herself to relax. If the image of Merco staring at her before she had darted from his house would only leave her mind long enough for her to think straight.

In spite of the cruelty the demon inflicted on her, the ache inside her for Merco wouldn't go away. For a moment she swore his scent saturated the air around her, the all-male musky aroma she'd experienced when she woke up in his bed. She glanced around the kitchen, taking in the white painted wooden cabinets and the simple beige countertops.

Turning her attention to Thena, her levelheaded friend who watched her with soft brown eyes, Naomi took a gulp of air, and exhaled slowly.

Thena was so pretty, and her life appeared tidy and in order. At the moment she had a silk scarf wrapped around her head, probably because she hadn't had time to do her hair before Naomi called her. The scarf was a pale pink and brought out the milk chocolate color of her skin nicely. Her features were smooth, her skin almost glowing as she focused on her short prayer. When she looked up, soft brown eyes like that of a doe's compelled Naomi to relax, share her story and hope Thena wouldn't think her nuts.

"I've been having these nightmares." Naomi sensed the demon stirring inside her when she started to tell Thena about him. "There is this creature..."

"You say a word about me, and you'll regret it." He'd returned, his hissing words making her blood run cold.

"He's a nasty creature, who touches me in my sleep." Naomi spoke quickly, fighting the pain that quickly traveled through her, all of her muscles suddenly clamping down hard as if she'd just worked all of them too hard. "He fucks me and threatens me," she added, wrapping her arms around her chest and doubling over in pain.

"Drink the tea." Thena had jumped up, bringing her a cup quickly.

Her friend hovered over her, holding the cup of steaming fluid to Naomi's lips. A pungent odor drafted to her nose, making her eyes water.

"It will help you think clearly. I promise." Thena's voice sounded far away.

Naomi focused on getting the demon to leave her alone. But he grew inside her, his anger resonating throughout her. She shivered in spite of her efforts.

Thena wrapped her arm around Naomi's shoulders, the warmth of her body seeping through her as the steam from the drink rose to her face. Thena pressed the cup to Naomi's lips. Naomi sipped, the hot fluid rushing down her throat while its vapors soaked through her, making her feel lightheaded for a moment.

"Something has crawled inside you. I feel your pain. Tell me more," Thena encouraged. "Open up so I can see it. I need to know so I can help get rid of it."

"Lately this creature comes to me while I'm awake." She wanted to blurt it all out, get the entire story told in one breath. "He is inflicting pain. He doesn't want me to tell you about him. God. This is so crazy."

"Drink the tea." Thena hurried to her cabinets, opening doors and pulling items out. "We will cast him out. If we try our hardest, I think this will work."

Hard bony fingers wrapped around her breasts, squeezing and kneading. Naomi swore the demon hovered over her now, hunching behind her, his repulsive deformed body pressed against her backside. She squeezed her eyes shut and took a large gulp of the tea. It burned down her throat while vapors drifted through her brain. She focused on them, fighting to rid the creature from her system.

Thena poured a mixture of herbs onto a flat metal tray and then lit them. A gray-blue smoke drifted up from the dried leaves and Thena ran her hands through it, spreading the smoke around them.

"We call on the gods to help us." Thena cupped her hands, lifting the smoke higher into the air.

A small knife rested on the table along with the other items Thena had pulled from her cabinets. Its blade was short and curved and her dark skin contrasted the ivory handle when she picked it up.

"This is my athame. I use it during all of my rituals." She held the knife out and then turned slowly, creating an imaginary circle by slicing the knife through the gray-blue smoke that hovered around them. "We seek the good. We cast out the bad. We seek the good. We cast out the bad." She repeated herself once more while Naomi watched.

Either the hot tea, or the smoke from the burning herbs, or maybe it was Thena's chanting, got to her. Naomi felt her muscles relax, found she could straighten. She took another sip of the strong tea, her thoughts suddenly lingering toward Merco. Did he partake in rituals like this?

"Asclepius, your medicinal strength we call forth." Thena had closed her eyes, holding the athame in her hand while she raised her arms, her lithe body stretching over Naomi. "Morpheus, you can move anything through dreams. Give us your power."

Swallowing, the lingering taste of the herbal tea in her mouth, Naomi focused on the smoke that swarmed around them, her thoughts on Merco. She wanted him to save her, rid her of this nasty demon, free her of her nightmares.

Thoughts of him casting this nasty demon out of her, forcing him to leave her alone, started a tingling between her legs. Dear God, she must be nuts.

A knocking sounded, firm and quick. It took Naomi a second to realize it was someone at Thena's door. Her heart raced from the intruding sound.

Thena turned her attention to her living area, her arms extended, the small knife blade catching the light and glistening. Her smooth chocolate skin glowed, her face flushed a rosy shade, making her look even more beautiful. Naomi stared up at her, thinking for a disillusioned moment that her friend looked just like a goddess, holding more power in her than she might realize.

"We can't be disturbed right now," she said, turning to face the smoke. "The door is locked. They'll go away."

But then both of them jerked their attention to the living area, the front door just out of view when the sound of the door opening made Naomi's heart lurch in her chest.

"Hello?" A man's voice, a low baritone, sent shivers through her.

Naomi recognized Merco immediately, as did her body. Every nerve ending inside her jumped to attention, her skin suddenly tingling all over.

Chapter Twelve

Merco recognized the commonly used herbs the second he walked into the house. The scent was no different from the old days, except today the women wouldn't be accused of being witches and stoned or hung.

It wasn't the herbs that hardened his insides, though. The fear and confusion that wrapped around Naomi pulled something from deep inside him. He'd given her space, let her run to sort through what she'd just seen. In no way would he lie about who he was. It seemed the longer he knew her, the more he wanted her to know who he was—what he was. He wanted her to know *him*.

But at the first sign of something out of the ordinary to her mortal mind, she'd fled. Merco stifled the heaviness that soaked through him that she might not want anything to do with him if she learned the truth and moved silently into the small house.

"Naomi." He entered the dining area but stopped before moving into the kitchen.

The young woman with her held a small ceremonial knife in her hand, moving the drifting smoke around as she called forth gods she knew nothing about. By the looks of her, they would be fools not to hurry to her aid.

But he only glanced at her for a moment. Naomi looked up at him from the chair she sat in, her hair twisted in ringlets and falling free over her shoulders and past her breasts. She took his breath away.

Damn it to all of the hells. It shouldn't be like this. She was a mere mortal.

No. Fuck that. Naomi was a person, albeit without powers, but she was a living creature who looked up at him confused and bewildered.

I will see to it personally nothing ever plagues you again. He let her know his thoughts—just a bit at a time. She would get accustomed to him.

"What? How did you do that?" Her eyes widened, her mouth forming an adorable circle as she looked up at him astonished.

"What did he do?" Her friend stared at him, knife in hand, although it would hardly serve as a decent weapon.

"He spoke to me...without moving his mouth," Naomi whispered, not taking her gaze from him.

"Oh." Her friend matched the hushed tone. "What did he say?"

"He said he would see to it that nothing ever plagued me again."

"Oh." Her friend already believed in him.

Naomi, on the other hand, looked skeptical. She studied him for a moment, wanting to question him, but not ready to hear the answers. He hated the doubt that clouded her eyes. No one would protect her better than he could, yet she'd run from him.

He couldn't stay away from her any longer, though. And he wouldn't take her wondering if she could trust him or not. She would see that he would be her strength. There was no other man for Naomi.

"Tell your friend thank you, and let's go." More than anything he needed to be alone with her right now.

The only way he could ensure that whatever tortured her left her alone is if he kept her with him—an idea that sounded strangely appealing. It wasn't like him to want to care for someone. That had never been in his nature.

She straightened at his words, but didn't rise. Instead something hardened in her expression, her lips pursing, looking full and moist. Her eyes sparkled with life like no other woman he'd known ever had. Tension riveted through him, the overwhelming desire to simply scoop her up and fade to another place making it real hard to focus on her words when she spoke.

"Merco. You don't simply prance into a stranger's house and insist that I leave with you." She tried to look stern, strong in front of her friend.

The flush crossing her face made his insides boil. Forcing his hands to stay by his side took more strength than he imagined. Throwing her over his shoulder crossed his mind.

But he saw straight through to the uncertainty that lay just underneath her calm expression. She placed her hands in her lap, but he didn't miss how her fingers shook. She was scared. Terrified, in fact. But her thoughts were easy to read. She wanted him to see her as strong, as an equal.

Silly woman. Why did her spunky defiance appeal to him so damned much?

"We're leaving." He reached for her, and at the same time nodded to her friend who still stared at him with a somewhat perplexed look on her face. "You may not realize it, but you have helped her."

She would never understand the powers she played with, but unlike so many humans, she worked with the gifts passed down from her ancestors and didn't simply play with them.

Naomi looked at his hand but still didn't move. He reached for her, touching her shoulder. The warmth of her skin traveled through him at a dangerous speed. Everything that was unique to her, her scent a mixture of perfume and soap, her natural red curls that traveled down her body, the softness of her body against his hand, every bit of it turned him on more than he thought a human capable of doing.

She stood slowly, hesitantly, her thoughts again easy to read when she worried what to say to her friend. Naomi wanted to be with him. That in itself brought his cock to life. But fear tormented her. Some entity plagued her mind, and watching Braze and Bridget disappear frightened her. He could easily put part of her fears to rest. Convincing Bridget it might be the right thing to do would be a challenge. But his friend's feisty woman didn't control Merco's actions. Naomi had a right to know what she had seen.

"This is the guy I told you about," Naomi began, her tone apologetic.

"From the coven?" Her friend let her gaze travel down him, appraising him. She then looked at Naomi. "Call me later."

Naomi nodded, standing slowly, unsteady for a moment. He wrapped his arm around her, her body fitting against his perfectly. He didn't say anything while he escorted her from the house. What he would do next would take all of his concentration to pull it off properly, and he didn't want to scare Naomi any further than she already had been.

"You know why I left your house," she said quietly as soon as the door to her friend's house closed behind them.

"Yes." He held her tight. No way would he let her go.

And she didn't fight him. Her attention was ahead of them, her expression hard to see from the locks that fell alongside her face. But even in her clothes that she'd slipped back on after waking up, and barefoot, he wanted her so desperately the pain began throbbing in his cock.

"They disappeared," she said, hesitantly.

"Yes." And they were going to also.

He held her close, knowing this was the best way for her to accept what she'd seen.

In the next instant, they were back in his living room.

"What?" Her fingernails dug into his chest. "Oh, shit."

Merco reached for her chin, lifting her face to his before she had a chance to react further. He'd just transported her from her friend's house to his living room and in a few minutes she would realize that was what Bridget and Braze had done, too. But before she panicked over the simple means of transportation, he had to taste her.

"Merco," she whispered, an urgency in her tone.

He captured any other words with his mouth, pressing against the wet softness of her lips.

She moaned into his mouth, dragging her fingernails up his shirt, gripping the material, holding on while she leaned into him.

Suddenly he was ravenous. He couldn't get enough of her. Leaning into her, crushing her against him, her full round breasts pressed against his chest, while one of her legs leaned in between his.

He held on to her tight, wanting more than anything to float up the stairs with her, fuck her good and hard until she accepted who he was.

"Damn it," he breathed into her mouth, realizing the direction of his thoughts.

In his urgency to protect her, discover what tormented her and get it the hell away from her, he'd forgotten his promise to himself. He wouldn't manipulate her with powers.

"What?" Her eyes were still closed. Her mouth was moist, parted, and her lips slightly swollen from his kiss.

His cock danced inside his jeans, demanding freedom.

"There are things you must know if I'm going to protect you." It was the only way.

It wasn't manipulation if she accepted the truth about him. She would stay with him of her own accord. He wouldn't coerce her thoughts.

"Sorry we're late." The voice behind Merco made Naomi jump, a small cry escaping her lips.

Merco turned and faced his friends, holding Naomi protectively to his side. She made no attempt to move.

"What are you two doing here?" He looked from Ace to Morph, two of his party buddies.

Both of them focused on Naomi. A pride he'd never experienced before washed through him. Their approving looks as they studied her made him pull her tighter into his arms. His friends over eternity knew she was mortal, saw her for what she was, and she appealed to them, too.

"We were called. And the lady who called us was so damned stunning there was no way to ignore her." Ace ran his fingers through his closely shaven beard and nodded to Naomi. "Your friend told us you were the one needing help."

"But it appears you are already doing your best to help her," Morph added, a gleam in his bright blue eyes.

Naomi straightened, obviously not feeling comfortable about being held so close to him in front of his friends. He hadn't proclaimed her his woman, but the thought crossed his mind with such intensity that he heard both men chuckle in their minds. He glared at the two of them.

"Morph. Ace. Allow me to present Naomi Lorghon." Merco didn't miss the look she gave him when he used her last name. She hadn't told him. He smiled down at her, releasing her but running his hand through her hair, loving its full texture.

She turned to the two men. "It's nice to meet you. Did Thena tell you that I was here?"

"She told us you were with Merco." Ace gave her his charming smile. "The two of you weren't too hard to find."

"What do you mean that she called you? Are you friends of hers, too?" She was trying to sort all of this out.

And there was no way she would pull it off. "Naomi. Like I mentioned before our guests arrived. There are things you need to know." Merco ignored the words of caution thought to him by both of his friends. "Your friend Thena didn't realize she was calling Ace and Morph. Most mortals are content to not believe in all that is out there. But your friend, and you as well, are willing to entertain the possibilities."

Naomi took a step away from him. He doubted she did it consciously. She crossed her arms, pushing those full breasts close together, the full bulges apparent even through her loose-fitting shirt. Her blue eyes glowed as her gaze darted from him to his friends, and then back to him again.

"Be careful, my friend." Morph stood maybe an inch taller than Merco, but didn't have his strength. He showed his concern for Naomi though, seeing that Merco felt something for her, and honoring that. Morph would defend Naomi now, too. "She is deeply tormented. I'm not sure how much she can handle at this point."

"What do you mean how much I can handle?" Naomi's temper flared, along with her fear, which hadn't completely left her yet. "Don't talk about me as if I am not here."

Her emotions were an open book, so raw and vulnerable that Merco knew his friend spoke with sincerity.

"My apologies," Morph said, nodding his head. "We only see how Merco cares for you. And any woman of Merco's we will also care for."

Naomi looked at Merco, giving him an odd look. He knew she wondered at the meaning of his friend's words. Again thoughts of what Bridget had told her entered her mind. Merco wouldn't elaborate on that at the moment. He sensed his friends' amusement, but also their concern.

"Did Thena tell you about the creature?" she whispered so softly her words were almost inaudible. Her breathing accelerated. "I'll do anything to get him out of my head."

Her lips parted while she took several breaths through her mouth. The mouth that he'd so recently ravished. Merco reached for her, knowing she meant her words.

And he would see to it that she didn't suffer, while whoever tortured her would suffer every second until they died.

Even now, as she looked up at him, confused and so damned vulnerable-looking, he could see the fighter in her. There was a determination in her to free herself of whatever tortured her. His heart swelled in his chest, creating a lump in his throat. Damn it if he didn't feel more than the urge to protect her, take care of her. He ached for her. Seeing her happy, relaxed, the haunted gaze in her eyes gone, meant more to him at that moment than anything had ever meant to him.

Not much scared him, but the thought that he might be falling in love with her terrified him.

"I can enter your dreams and take care of whatever disturbs you." Morph gave her a gallant bow.

Naomi cocked her head at him. "And I can just imagine how you would offer to do that." She turned an accusing gaze toward Merco. "Bridget told me..."

But Merco didn't care what Bridget told her. Other than to stay the fuck away. He reached for her, grabbing her wrist, and pulling her to him before she could resist. His friends could be gone in an instant, and she didn't need any more trauma today.

Looking over her head, he gave his friends a mental warning to give him some time, not to push her before she was ready to handle what had to be done.

"Let me talk things over with Naomi. I'll give you two a call." He listened to both of them share their thoughts, their fond jeers as they teased him of finally finding a woman who would make a decent man out of him.

He smiled as he watched the two of them disappear.

"Go ahead and see yourselves out," he said for Naomi's benefit after they had gone.

He held her when she would have turned around to tell them goodbye.

"It's me you need to focus on," he told her, watching the emotion swirl in her alluring blue eyes. "I'm far from done with you."

"What were they talking about?" Her curiosity was piqued, while so many thoughts raced through her head.

He held on to the one where she wondered if they shared women. It didn't surprise him Bridget would have told her that. Naomi wasn't at all sure about that possibility. Her hesitant reaction to the thought was as clear as if she'd voiced it out loud. But she couldn't let the idea go. And for now, it distracted her from whatever tortured her mind.

"They are my friends. And they will do whatever I ask." And he would do the same for them. It had always been like that since they were boys. "Right now, I think we need to help you relax. Then I might call them back."

"Why would you call them back?" A pink flush spread across her cheeks and she looked down, while her hands traced electric trails up his chest.

His skin shivered against her touch, although he was far from cold. Heat rushed through him at a dangerous speed. Her thoughts distracted him, and although he knew he should stay out of her head, he enjoyed the fact that she mused over fucking all three of them. It terrified and excited her all at once.

Merco fought the urge to make her clothes disappear. It was so natural to use powers to seduce a woman. But he was up to the challenge of winning her on her own terms.

Undressing her by hand would be just as pleasurable. His friends were right, giving her bits of knowledge at a time would be best.

"Something torments you. And I can't see it. But I think they might be able to help." He ran his hands over her head, tangling his fingers in her hair and pulling enough that she looked up at him. "When the time is right, we will invite them back. And we will free your mind of whatever tortures you."

"When the time is right?" She didn't fight him, but let her head fall back, the blue in her eyes glowing with sensuality. "When will that be?"

"You aren't tormented right now." He brushed the back of his hands down the front of her shirt, feeling her nipples harden to stone when he grazed over them.

"Not by that creature," she said, biting her lower lip while her eyes fluttered shut.

Lowering his mouth to her neck, he ran his teeth and tongue over the soft curve there. She gasped, her body jumping against the sudden touch. Merco thought he would explode from the fire that suddenly rushed through him. Never had he experienced such sudden rush of need from such a simple act.

Women of his own creation did everything because he commanded it, down to the softest of moans. Mortals were easy to figure out because their thoughts were so exposed.

But when he'd touched her just now, Naomi hadn't been ready for it. She hadn't given it any thought, just reacted. The spontaneity of her sexy moan was enough to harden his cock to stone. He pulled her against him, nibbling his way down to her collarbone. His throbbing shaft pulsated against her body.

"You are tormenting me," he told her.

Her breathing increased. "What...what are you going to do about it?"

There were still fears. He would do anything to wipe them away. But at the moment a powerful lust, a craving as strong as his, consumed her.

"I'm going to fuck you every way imaginable," he said, biting at her shirt, pulling it away from her body.

Naomi yanked on his clothes, fisting the material in her hand. More than anything he fought the hard to kick habit of simply making her clothes vanish. Or possibly grabbing her shirt, shredding it like it was paper. Thinking was a chore, but he forced himself to lift her shirt, sliding it up and exposing her creamy white skin.

She let go of him, extending her arms, allowing him to raise the material until he'd pulled it free from her body. Her full round breasts were perky, perfectly shaped, her nipples hard gems.

"I can imagine many ways of fucking," she said when he dropped her shirt to the floor.

"Let me guess your favorite position." He stared into her blue eyes, the color darkening while he probed deep into her thoughts. "Up against the wall, huh?"

Her cheeks darkened a rosy color, while she nibbled at her lip and suddenly looked terribly guilty.

"How the hell do you do that? You are reading my mind." She shook her head, her breath coming long and hard.

He reached for her sweat pants, tugging at the elastic waistline. She took a staggered step into him. Her lust drugged her, excitement radiating from her sultry body. The fact that he could tell her thoughts excited her. She should be terrified. But her lust overcame her, and he really liked that about her.

"Get used to it, my dear," he told her, undoing her pants and sliding them over the curve of her hips. "Just know you will always have it just the way you want it. I will always know just what pleases you."

"You make it sound like we are a couple." She looked down quickly after speaking.

He knew she hadn't meant to say that out loud, and the fact that she had, embarrassed her. It was selfish of him, but he remained quiet, not commenting, and refusing to admit that it embarrassed him, too. The statement had made their relationship sound rather permanent.

All he should do right now was focus on fucking her.

Chapter Thirteen

Naomi stood naked before Merco, alone in his large living room. It was so fucking hot to be exposed for him like this. His hands were all over her, caressing and exploring and sending her over the edge with a hard-core need.

She wanted him to fuck her so bad she could hardly think straight.

What the hell was wrong with her?

Other than being possessed by some crazed creature, she was allowing some man, who did things that just weren't right—weren't normal—to seduce her once again. And she wanted more.

"I want your clothes off, too." It was her voice speaking but she couldn't believe how brazen she sounded.

This wasn't like her. Hell, yes, she enjoyed sex. But Merco brought out something in her that she didn't know existed. The urge to be daring, to speak her mind, to tell him what she wanted—this wasn't how she usually was.

Not that she had drop-dead gorgeous men seducing her on a regular basis.

Merco ran his hands down her arms and took her hands in his. "Undress me," he told her.

Oh, hell, yeah.

Her mouth grew dry, her breath coming in pants, as she took his shirt and raised it over his head, exposing so many rippling muscles. Her pussy constricted, cream flowing over her swollen flesh. The pounding need between her legs made her crave to be touched there.

She bit her lip. More. She needed to see more of him—all of him. After fumbling with his jeans for a moment, her fingers suddenly incapable of the most basic task, he took over, quickly sliding out of his jeans.

All she could do was stare at his swollen cock, long and thick as it stood at attention.

God. She needed that inside her now or she would die. The pain pulsated through her, starting in her pussy and working its way deep into her gut. A twisting, driving ache for that hard cock to be shoved inside her, to quench the growing thirst that burst throughout her.

"Merco." She sounded like she was begging, and all she could manage was to say his name.

He took her, his grip hard and determined, and turned her back to him, pushing her up against the wall. Just as she'd imagined. What was it about this man?

Right now there was no way she could dwell on how easily he knew what she wanted. And she sure as hell wasn't going to think about how they'd gotten here from Thena's house. The only thing she wanted to focus on right now was having his cock deep inside her.

She stretched out her arms, pressing her palms against the smooth wall and running them against it. Arching her back, she offered her ass.

Merco had his hands on her instantly, kneading her ass, encouraging her to spread her legs while he pulled her to him. The head of his cock pushed against her, velvety yet so hard, a weapon disguised as pleasure.

His thumbs pressed against the tender entrance of her ass. Shivers rushed through her as she closed her eyes, running her tongue over her lips and enjoying the many sensations that traveled through her.

She wanted him in her, forcing his way toward that special spot that would put her over the edge. He had what it took and right now she needed it more than anything. She wouldn't focus on anything else. Spread-eagled against his wall in such a vulnerable position, she felt brazen, alive.

"Fuck me," she breathed, again wondering at her willingness to be so open, so daring with how she spoke to him.

Merco plunged inside her cunt with so much force her entire body smashed into the wall. Its cool smooth surface did nothing to soothe the fire that shot through her.

"God. Yes." She pressed her cheek against the hard plaster.

His cock slid deep inside her, easing past soaked and swollen muscles, caressing her insides with his velvety hardness.

"That's it, baby. Take all of me." He stretched her ass, pulling against her flesh while he thrust even further inside her. "Oh, you are so fucking hot."

He hadn't reached the spot that needed him the most before he began sliding out of her, leaving her craving him even more.

"Merco," she gasped.

And then he drove inside her again. Thrusting with enough strength that she feared her hipbones would bruise against the wall, he impaled her with his cock. She swore it had grown in size over the past couple of seconds. Pressure soared clear up to her belly button.

Naomi cried out, unable to stop herself.

Hard and deep. Quick and fast. Merco fucked her with an aggressiveness no man had taken with her before. He wasn't gentle. Gripping her ass, he plunged into her, pounding her again and again until white light splattered before her eyes.

She exploded, working hard to breathe so she could ride out her orgasm. She didn't want it to end, didn't want him to stop the quick and fierce way he took her. Never had sex been so damned good.

And then he slowed the movement, reaching around and gliding his hands over her moist skin. His legs bent against hers, while he pulled her back, adjusting himself so he eased slowly deep inside her.

"You are so fucking perfect." He pressed her against him, his cock buried deep inside her.

She let her head fall back, arching against him, freeing herself from the stability of the wall. The moisture from their bodies helped them to cling to each other, their overheated skin melding as one while his hips continued to work, a slow sultry movement. His cock glided in and out of her, allowing her to ride out her orgasm and still feel the urgent craving for a more intense satisfaction.

She almost told him he was perfect, that no man had ever made her feel like this. But he seemed so damned convinced he could read her thoughts, there was really no reason to talk. Silently she begged for more.

Butterflies fluttered in her gut when he chuckled, icy chills rushing over her overheated body.

"I'm not sure I want to know what is so funny," she gasped, craving to come again, and not wanting to dwell on how damned spooky he could be.

She didn't want to think about that right now. The demon that tortured her didn't seem to want anything to do with her when she was fucking Merco. And as far as she was concerned Merco could keep up what he was doing for hours and she would be more than delighted.

"You already know," he told her, finalizing his words with a quick hard thrust.

"Shit!" she cried out, her body convulsing with an unexpected orgasm.

She couldn't ride it out before he pulled free from her, grabbing her and turning them around so that she fell toward the coffee table. She felt like a rag doll, incapable of stopping him from moving her into whatever position he desired. When he pressed against her ass, she reached forward, her hands slapping the cool surface of the coffee table.

Naomi screamed when he went down behind her, thrusting his tongue deep into her cunt.

"Damn, woman, you are on fire." His tongue worked magic over her swollen cunt, stroking and caressing the tortured flesh that he had just thoroughly fucked.

"That is good. Yes. Just like that." She'd never told a man how to please her before.

In the few times in her far past that she'd been with a man, she had taken what she could get. The thought of instructing, letting him know what to do to her, required more nerve than she'd ever mustered.

Yet she couldn't stop herself. "Merco. More."

His large hands, so sure and confident, pressed against her flesh, tugging and stretching while his mouth worked pure pleasure against her fiery entrance.

Her hair fell around her, while she pressed her palms against the glass surface of the coffee table. The pull on her inner thighs burned, but she stretched her legs as far as she could, wanting more of what he was doing to her.

And then his tongue thrust into her sensitive ass. Nerve endings sprang to life and she jerked at the incredibly intimate act. Her body convulsed. No one had ever tongue-fucked her ass. She couldn't breathe, couldn't think, couldn't move while he daringly committed the most pleasurable act on her that she'd ever had in her life.

"You would explode if I fucked you here," he told her, his breath burning against her moist and exposed ass.

"Oh," she murmured, unable to think, far from able to respond while he did what he did to her.

"Tell me you want it here." He circled the sensitive flesh with the rough texture of his tongue.

Fire scourged through her. Pressure built with more intensity than it had when he'd fucked her pussy.

She couldn't speak. Turning her head simply caused her hair to fall further over her face. Her muscles constricted, her entire body one overactive nerve ending.

"Tell me," he told her again, determination in his voice.

Chills of excitement rushed through her.

"Yes. Okay." She couldn't have formed a complete sentence if her life depended on it.

"Tell me," he said again.

Damn it. He wouldn't let her simply enjoy the act. He wanted her to think, too. How could she possibly have a conversation with him when he was doing this to her with his tongue?

"Merco," she pleaded, squeezing her eyes shut, all of her attention on the slow, torturous strokes of his tongue against her incredibly sensitive ass.

He stabbed her again, the moisture from his mouth oozing over her ass, the small hole soaked from his focused administrations.

"You will tell me." He wouldn't let it be. His husky baritone rushed over her skin.

She would die. Never would she be able to think clearly again. Blood rushed through her, heating her brain. Her muscles strained, her body quivering with a need for more.

"Yes," she cried out. "Fuck my ass."

He adjusted himself quickly, his hard cock suddenly where his mouth had been. Her soaked ass greeted the swollen head, his velvety hardness sliding over her moist skin.

And when he pressed into her, stretching the prepared opening of her ass, the pressure building inside her threatened to explode, erupting with more intensity than she could possibly handle.

His cock pushed into her ass, suddenly filling her with his hardness while her legs quivered, her muscles threatening to collapse underneath her. Merco tightened his grip on her, a growl escaping him while he plunged into the tight crevice and fucked her ass.

Nothing compared to it. The fiery pain mixed with the most incredible pleasure while she collapsed to the coffee table, crying out as a dam burst inside her.

Somehow she managed to keep her legs straight, enjoying the long thickness of him while he stroked her tight hole, caressing the most sensitive muscles as he glided in and out of her.

"Damn it, Naomi." The roughness of his voice put her over the edge. "You've got a fucking perfect ass."

She couldn't talk. Her breath came in gasps. She stretched into him, overwhelmed with the orgasm that passed through her while at the same moment pressure built inside. She came, and then came again. Nothing had ever felt so damned perfect.

"Yes." He growled again, a primal sound, bellowing from deep inside him while he plunged one last time, his cock pulsating inside her while he spilled his seed.

His growl vibrated through her, adding to the intensity of her climax. She'd never known anal sex could be this good. No one ever could have made her believe such a carnal act would leave her numb, tingling, wanting to cry from the sheer joy of it

The hot fluid coated her ass, soothing the fire that he'd created there.

Naomi collapsed, the coolness of the glass against her cheek all she could focus on. No man had ever confused her more, yet brought her such perfection. Merco was the most incredible man she had ever experienced.

For a moment she thought she might pass out. There was no way she could move. Her body had never felt more sated.

And then Merco lifted her, pulling her backwards until he had picked her up into his arms.

"Come here," he whispered.

She turned contentedly, curling into his chest while he cradled her against him. The hard beat of his heart and the heat of his body saturated through her.

"I doubt I could go anywhere if I wanted to," she told him, hardly able to catch her breath.

Merco chuckled. "You, my dear, are going to take a bath."

She looked up at him, wondering at how sensitive he could be to her needs at times. A hot bath sounded absolutely perfect. For the first time in quite a while she was at peace, comfortable, and very happy.

The demon creature seemed to be gone. But she wouldn't dwell on that right now. Good riddance. All she would focus on was the aftermath of their sex. Her body ached, pulsing with an intense satisfaction. Even the burning in her ass and her pussy from such hard sex felt good.

Merco didn't look down at her but focused ahead as he carried her up the stairs. She remembered coming down these stairs earlier today and seeing Bridget and Braze disappear. His expression remained solemn as he moved easily until he reached the upstairs hallway, not jostling her once as he moved to the bedroom where she'd slept that morning.

"What is it about you?" she asked, knowing she wouldn't get an answer.

Like anyone could answer a question like that.

"I'm not like anyone you've ever known." His answer was perfect, yet a mystery.

"You're right about that," she told him, more than confused.

The slightest amount of trepidation seeped through her. He wasn't like anyone she'd ever known. He was too damned sexy. And sexy men didn't seek her out. She was normal, ordinary. She wasn't a flirt. And she was intelligent. Those qualities just never seemed to attract the overly cocky, gorgeous men.

Yet Merco had come to her. He was strange, to say the least. But that fascinated her. Terrified her, but yet appealed to her at the same time. She really was a nutcase.

When they entered the bathroom the large oval-shaped tub was full of steamy water, bubbles threatening to spill over.

"Damn." She shouldn't have been surprised. But her heart started a hard beat while her stomach twisted in knots.

Merco stepped easily over the edge and submerged into the hot water, holding onto her firmly while he adjusted her on his lap. The hot sudsy water rushed up around her, steam and the perfect amount of heat enveloping her.

Her long hair clung instantly to her as she found herself suddenly situated on his lap, the hot water covering her up to her chest.

"Who filled this bath?" she asked him, wondering why she hadn't thought that they might not have been alone in the house.

The thought that someone else could have been there, able to watch them in the living room if they had chosen, sent a rush of embarrassed heat through her.

"I did," he told her simply.

"You did?" she asked, turning to look into that incredibly calm-looking face.

"Yes. I did," he said with finality.

She stared at him, an uncomfortable emptiness sinking through her. A slow lump began in her gut while she studied the hard line of his jaw, the determined look on his face.

"You filled this tub?" she asked again, her mind working to figure out how he could have done that.

There simply was no way he could have drawn a hot bath when he'd been with her ever since they were at Thena's. Her heart raced, a cold flush creeping over her skin. She shouldn't be scared. But what kind of man was Merco?

Merco raised his arm, suds dripping off of his dark skin. Muscles stretched under his skin as he brushed her soaked hair over her shoulders. The touch was so intimate, so relaxed, the way a lover would treat another lover. Yet this man was a stranger, full of mysteries that she couldn't figure out. She simply stared at him, ignoring the gesture.

"Merco. How could you have filled this tub?"

"I willed it to be filled. Just as I willed us here from your friend's house. And the same way that Bridget and Braze willed themselves home from my living room earlier today." His gaze never left her face.

He waited, staring at her, waiting for her reaction. And all she could do was stare at him. There was no way to react to such a preposterous statement.

"What the hell are you talking about?" Suddenly the heat from the water made her dizzy. Everything around her seemed to be spinning, her insides included. "You make it sound like you are magic."

Chapter Fourteen

"Magic is a human word." He waited for her to explode. Until then he would give her the simple truth. In spite of the consequences that he was sure would hit him sooner or later, she deserved that much from him. "I am an immortal, just as Bridget and Braze are, just as my friends you met earlier are. We are elders from a place called Hedel."

When she said nothing, he stretched out in the tub underneath her, adjusting her against him. The hot water felt damned good, but not as good as her soft curves did resting on top of him.

She remained relaxed over him only for a minute, though. Slowly she straightened until she slid down him, her soft ass caressing his cock until she sat in between his legs.

Hunched in the center of the tub, the deep water covering her to her breasts, he watched her while ringlets of steam curled around them.

"That's not funny," she said finally, her lips pursing while frustration brushed over her face.

"It wasn't meant to be." He watched while she struggled with a mixture of emotions. "It's the truth."

Naomi stood, the water creating waves with her quick action. Quickly she stepped out of the bath. Standing in the middle of his bathroom, water dripping from her naked body, she crossed her arms and glared at him.

"If you are in any way responsible for the demon creature who tortures me in my dreams, I swear you will live to regret it." She turned on him, yanking open the bathroom door, and slamming it loudly behind her.

Every muscle inside him clenched in outrage. His fiery redhead had a temper. Well, he wouldn't be pushed around. No woman ever stormed out on him, especially in the wake of some of the best sex he'd ever had.

Merco leapt from the tub, drying himself with a thought while he raced out of the bathroom after her. She was already down the stairs and in the living room, struggling to pull her clothes on over her wet body.

He allowed a towel to appear and handed it to her, knowing she was too upset to notice it had appeared out of nowhere.

"I'm not responsible for whatever is torturing you," he told her calmly.

She yanked the towel from him and wrapped it around her damp skin, giving up on her clothes for the moment. Staring at him, her blue eyes showing her tortured pain, she ran her tongue over her lips.

"Well, if you are magic, make it go away," she told him defiantly.

In all of his dealings with humans, none had ever stood up to him the way she did now. His heart swelled, an ache that grew and spread throughout him while he reached for her. She didn't come to him, but stood her ground. He went to her instead.

"Naomi," he whispered, brushing her wet hair to the side of her face. "I don't understand why I can't see what tortures you. Something powerful has mastered hiding from the gods."

She shook her head, squeezing her eyes closed for a moment before looking him straight in the eye.

"You're scaring me," she confessed. "And I want to run from you. But when I'm with you, he leaves me alone."

That told him this creature of hers knew who he was, feared him, knew he would wipe it out of existence if he found him in her. Anger swirled through him, his muscles hardening with determination that she would not leave his side.

"I'm going to take care of you."

She was worth fighting for, and it would be worth her accepting who he was just to have her by his side—always. The realization that he wanted that created a tightening in his gut that he hadn't expected. Naomi needed him. He'd already accepted that. But the thought that he needed her, too, meant accepting what he already knew to be the truth. He loved her. And for the duration of her life, he would be with her. If she would have him, he wanted her as his wife.

The elders would throw a fit. Gods didn't take humans as mates. History had shown what happened when such a matrimonial fusion occurred. Their offspring would be outcasts. Neither would be fully accepted in the other's world. But leaving her, allowing her to lead out her life without him, find a good human man to take as a husband, didn't sit well with him at all. No other man would call Naomi his woman. Not ever. If she would accept that he was a god, then he would willingly stand beside her, enjoy every moment of her mortal life.

She turned from him, keeping the towel around her but using the corner of it to dry her hair. Just watching her long slender legs, so creamy white, and her small feet walk across his carpet, made him want her all over again. Standing there naked, he felt the pressure build in his groin, his sated cock do a small dance of anticipation at the thought of fucking her again.

"So you can make sure that this *thing* never bothers me again?" Her voice was soft, unsure.

He knew she wanted to trust him, but he asked a lot of her. She was open to new things, but he'd thrown the unbelievable out at her, and could tell she wasn't ready to believe him. Only out of desperation did she ask him that.

"My friends who were here," he began carefully, knowing much more information might have her running out of his door again. "Morph and Ace will be able to help. But they won't until you trust them."

She turned around and looked at him, a multitude of questions in her expression.

"Until I have your trust," he added, watching her.

She nodded, although he was aware of her confusion. She needed time, and he would give her that. But she would stay with him until she accepted how things would be.

He stepped to the side, gesturing to the stairs. "Go upstairs. Enjoy the bath. When you come down, I will have a meal ready for us."

She chewed her lip for a moment, her gaze traveling down him. She enjoyed the view and didn't want to leave him. He offered her security and she wanted that. As she had told him, he kept her nightmares away. Now to convince her that she wanted to be with him for more reasons than that.

Without a word, she walked past him, and went up the stairs slowly, not looking back at him while she returned to the hot bath waiting upstairs.

Leaving her to her own thoughts for a bit would do her some good. Merco knew he'd given her a lot of information, and she wouldn't accept it without thinking it over. He padded quietly into his kitchen, not surprised to see Ace and Morph making themselves at home.

"Where'd you find her?" Ace asked. He sat cross-legged on the middle of Merco's kitchen table, idly flipping through one of the magazines Merco had left there.

"At one of their covens." Merco walked over to his counter, staring at the clean surface until a large silver platter appeared, a variety of sliced meats and cheeses on it.

"Oh, ho!" Ace whooped, giving Merco a slap on the back. "She is one of those who thinks herself a witch."

Merco shook his head, creating another wooden cutting board with fresh sliced bread on it.

"She was simply curious. Naomi has no powers." He turned to face his friends, knowing they would always be there for him when he needed them. "But she does have something plaguing her. And I don't like the fact that I can't see who it is."

He quickly filled them in on what he knew about her nightmares. "She doesn't want to talk about it. And I think it's because whoever is torturing her is threatening her if she speaks."

His two friends grew serious.

"If she doesn't trust us, we can't help her," Ace pointed out.

Both of them looked at him. They weren't telling him anything he didn't already know.

"She is scared." And that bothered him more than anything. What he wouldn't do to squeeze the life out of whoever terrified her.

"Her tormentor is satisfied that she will be loyal to him and not speak. If she were to describe him, give us a clue, we would know who it was." Morph reached behind Merco, stealing a piece of cheese. "You need to gain her trust."

"I know that." Merco balled his hands into fists, the urge to crush something getting the best of him. "And I'm working on it."

"You realize the coven will be pissed when they learn you've told a human about your true nature." Ace changed the subject. One might not notice by his relaxed position on Merco's table, but he was the serious one, always cautious with his actions.

"I don't give a damn what the elders of the coven think." And he didn't. All that mattered to him right now was convincing Naomi that he was the only one who could help her. "I will gain her trust. And I will know when I have it."

The other two nodded, understanding. In the past, the true way they knew if a woman would be loyal to them, was if they could share her, and she would come back to them. He knew Naomi wasn't ready for that right now. But in time, with a little effort, he would see if she would give herself to him completely, allowing him to share her and offer her greatest gift to his friends.

His two friends disappeared when they heard Naomi coming down the stairs. He carried the two trays to the table, focusing first on her feet when she entered the room. Placing the trays down, he took his time taking her in. Even her feet turned him on. This just wasn't like him.

But his body tightened, the air squeezing from his lungs when his gaze traveled up her.

"I hope you don't mind." She stroked the silky material of the shirt she'd found in his closet. "I didn't feel like putting those clothes on again after bathing."

"It's never looked better," he told her, and meant it. Even in the oversized shirt, every button buttoned, she made his heart stop beating.

She allowed a small smile, and looked down. But her guard was up. There were things on her mind, a lot of things, and she didn't know how to approach him with her many questions.

"Have a seat." The first thing he needed to do was make her surroundings comfortable, like home. She would open up sooner that way. "I wasn't sure what you liked."

She sat down, her slender legs bare under the long shirt that flowed around her thighs. Bending her over the table and burying himself in her heat sounded a hell of a lot better than a sandwich. His cock moved to life at the thought, but he ordered himself to behave. For now, they would talk.

"This is fine." She clasped her hands in her lap, her head lowered.

Merco brought a couple plates to the table and then wineglasses. Turning to the counter he reached out and picked up a bottle of wine that wasn't there a second ago. It had been a last-minute thought. She might relax more after a glass or two. Although he risked upsetting her more if she noticed the action, the soothing alcohol might be well worth it.

She was still looking down when he popped the cork and poured the rippling dark fluid into each glass. He placed her glass in front of her, distracted by how her hair curled into perfect ringlets when it was damp. The dark amber hair contrasted her creamy complexion perfectly.

"Drink," he told her.

Obediently she picked up the glass and pressed her lips to the glass. He watched her slender throat move as she swallowed, remembering how she tasted there, the silky feel of her skin. A swelling moved through him, protective, demanding, carnal. He took a gulp from his own glass and then sat down across from her.

"I suppose you made all of this food magically appear." She reached for a slice of bread and placed it on her plate.

Then taking a piece of beef, she tore a bit of it free and put it in her mouth. Her gaze shot up to him, her fingers still at her lips while her blue eyes searched his face.

He didn't see any reason to answer that question. She knew the answer already. "Tell me about this creature who plagues you," he said instead, changing the subject.

Her eyes darkened, her forehead wrinkling with worry while she studied him for a moment, taking her time in answering. She was scared and he hated that. Gaining her trust would take time, but he had plenty of that.

"He doesn't want me to talk about him," she whispered, fear in her tone.

"I realize that. That tells me that he knows who I am, and he fears me." He watched her eyes widen, but only for a moment. Slowly the wrinkles in her forehead disappeared. "Tell me what you can about him."

She took another bite of the meat, chewing it slowly and then swallowing. Her tongue darted over her lips. His cock surged to life, aching for the feel of that soft tongue over his sensitive cock head. But even more, the way she sorted through her thoughts, determined that telling him was in her best interest, turned him on more than her actions.

This was terrifying. What she thought even excited him. Something about this woman drove him mad with need, with a primal desire to take care of her, see to her needs, ensure she would always be safe. He waited while she took a slow breath and then let it out silently.

"He is disgusting-looking," she began, speaking so softly he almost didn't hear her. "When he touches me, I want to puke."

"How does he touch you?" Everything hardened inside him. Just the thought of someone violating her had him seeing red.

Those soft eyes, a beautiful lusty blue, gazed up at him, her lashes fluttering while she ran her tongue over her lips.

"He touches me sexually, plays with me, gropes and fondles me whenever I try to fall asleep."

"And that is why you called out for me that first night."

She nodded, not taking her gaze from him.

"I didn't think you would believe me." She reached for a piece of cheese and her hands trembled. "I didn't think anyone would believe me."

"Tell me more about what he looks like, what he says to you." He ached to move to her, take her in his arms, assure her that she would never be tortured again.

But this would take time. At least for now, she was talking to him, sharing with him what she hadn't shared with anyone else. Well, she'd told her girlfriend, and at least that much had drawn their attention.

"When I saw you downtown, in that shop," she began, tearing at the bread now and not looking at him. "I saw a figurine that looked exactly like him. It scared the hell out of me."

Merco had reached for bread and stopped in mid-action. He remembered that night, watching her walk distracted along the street, preventing the car from hitting her, and then the figurine of the demon leader mysteriously appearing in Marlita's shop. There was no way she would stock such an item, yet there it had been. And it had scared the shit out of Naomi.

He wanted to kick himself. At the time he'd been so focused on seeing if he could seduce her without powers that he hadn't bothered to see the obvious. But the demon leader was…

"Are you sure it looked exactly like him?" he asked, needing to be sure. Fury surged through him over the possibilities here.

Naomi nodded. "At first glance I thought it was him." She shuddered, fear wrapping around her as she leaned back in her chair, wrapping her arms around her waist. She'd apparently lost interest in her food.

Merco stood, his anger accelerating tenfold. The demon leader had been destroyed. Or that was what he thought had happened when Bridget escaped from his grasp in the hells. Merco had been there to witness it. He and Braze had shown up right after she'd made him disappear, seconds too late from witnessing the despicable creature's destruction.

And Bridget had gone into the hells to save Naomi. Albeit Merco hadn't known her then, he knew that Bridget chased after her when the demon leader had captured her. And Bridget had saved her, then wiped her mind clear of all memory of the horrible experience.

Somehow…something had gone terribly wrong.

"What is it?" Naomi had stood, and reached for him when he turned to her. But then she pulled her hand back, unsure.

Fire rushed over him, egging on the temper that threatened to unleash. Muscles clenched painfully. He inhaled slowly before something in the kitchen broke. He wouldn't let her see his outrage. Never did he want to see Naomi afraid to touch him. He forced his temper at bay.

"When was the first time you ever saw this creature? Think carefully." He took her hand that she'd pulled from him, focusing on the softness of her skin. She was so fragile, yet enduring so much silently.

She didn't pull her hand away but looked down while he stroked her skin with his thumb. A different kind of burning began from the friction touching her skin, stroking it, feeling her soft heat flush through his system.

"The first time…" she hesitated, relaxing her hand in his, brushing her fingers ever so slightly over the top of his hand. The hairs on his skin stood at attention, electricity shocking him from her soft alluring touch. "The first time was in a dream."

But she wasn't sure. Her thoughts were a clutter of confusion as she frowned, trying to remember. Somehow whatever spell Bridget had cast on her, making her forget the torturous time she had spent in the hells, was wearing off. This wasn't heard of. Most mortals had no way of controlling the extremity of anything cast upon them. His heart leapt at the thought that Naomi had more insight than most, that her consciousness had opened fractions further than most humans, allowing her to control her environment the way most mortals couldn't.

"You've only seen him in dreams," he prompted, aching to plunge into her thoughts, tear through her darkest memories to make sure for himself.

But he wouldn't do that to her. He couldn't do that. In spite of how desperately the truth mattered, Naomi was a fragile soul at the moment. He worried if he conjured up too many dark memories by sorting through them that she might not be able to handle it.

If the demon leader had somehow managed to traipse through her most concealed thoughts, though, he could have surfaced images that she was supposed to forget.

He'd tightened his grip on her hand without realizing it, his own thoughts plaguing him to the point where he needed to strike out, to release the anger he refused to allow to surface.

"You're hurting me," she said quietly. "What is it?"

He let go of her hand instantly, angry at himself for not being able to better curb his growing rage. Naomi didn't need to see the danger that she was in. If the demon leader somehow had housed himself inside her, her entire existence was at risk. This was more serious than he had first thought.

"I will never hurt you. Come here." He couldn't keep his hands off of her. Reaching for her, wrapping her into his embrace, he inhaled her clean scent, the fresh smell of soap and the warmth of her body. "I'm going to get that bastard out of you. Do you understand me? But it's going to take your trust—your complete trust and faith in me. I can't act until I know that you will allow me to do whatever is necessary."

Chapter Fifteen

Something wasn't right here. Naomi sat on Merco's bed, a bed they had yet to fuck in, and stared at the phone in her hand. She'd just called work and used a few of her vacation days to take some time off. Then she'd called Thena, who thought all of this was a great adventure. Now she needed to call Bridget.

Even though she'd just showered, and had a wonderful night's sleep in Merco's arms, she couldn't get her mind to work. The godawful creature hadn't bothered her, but she couldn't escape the feeling that he was lingering, plotting and planning something terrible.

"Just great, now I'm trying to get into its head," she moaned, kicking her bare feet over the side of the king-sized bed.

"Did you say something, miss?" The older man who Merco said would be here if she needed anything while he was gone, stuck his head in through the door.

"I'm just mumbling to myself," she admitted, suddenly feeling he had been listening at the door. "Did Merco say when he would be back?"

"It's hard telling with that man." He ran thick pudgy fingers through his close-shaven salt-and-pepper beard.

The man reminded her of an old retired lumberjack. He was thick, not fat, but more than likely in his youth had been quite muscular. His wrists looked bigger than her forearms. There was a pleasant twinkle in his eye when he gave her a closed lip smile.

Naomi stood, feeling a bit weird in the oversized shirt and long underwear Merco told her to put on while he was gone. They fit her perfectly, making her wonder where they'd come from.

Had he conjured them up just for her? That thought was too much to fathom. But thinking that they'd been left here by some other woman didn't sit well with her at all.

"I don't remember your name," she said, leaving the large bedroom while the older man pushed the door open further, allowing her to pass.

"Everyone calls me Birk," he said from behind her, his footsteps heavy and solid as he followed her slowly down the stairs.

Naomi walked into the living room, stopping in front of one of the large windows, an incredible view of a perfect yard laid out before her. Again she wondered where Merco had gone. He had been so vague, simply instructing that she stay here and he'd be back shortly.

"You've got yourself into quite a situation, haven't you?" he said, sounding concerned.

Naomi turned around, giving him her complete attention. Her heart leapt at the realization that possibly she could gain some helpful information about Merco from this man.

"You've known Merco a while?" she inquired, hoping she didn't sound too anxious.

"All his life." He stroked his beard, staring at her through squinted eyes. He was relaxed, in control, and watchful. "And I've never known him to narrow in on one lady before. I'm not sure if that is lucky for you or not."

With that he smiled, but his expression remained serious. And his gaze remained attentive. Even now, with his round potbelly stretching against his flannel shirt, she imagined he was still in his prime. Something about him gained her respect. He was kind, yet alert to everything around him.

Her tummy twisted in a mixture of excitement and fear. "He has told me some strange things."

Birk raised a bushy eyebrow, his pale blue eyes piercing through her. She felt her mouth go dry as if she'd just said the wrong thing.

"Oh, really?" Again his stubby fingers stroked his beard while he took a step closer, walking around her as if appraising her. "And what are these strange things?"

Naomi waved her hand in the air, dismissing the question. A wave of uneasiness rushed through her.

"They don't make sense to me. I'm sure it's nothing." She turned away from his scrutinizing gaze, her mouth suddenly dry.

Maybe a glass of water would help.

Birk followed her into the kitchen, stopping in the doorway while she helped herself to a glass out of the cabinet. There was very little food in the house, half of the cabinets empty as if they had never been used.

As if he didn't need to stock groceries but simply made food appear when he wanted it. She saw no signs of the leftover meat, cheese or bread he had fed her the day before. Her heart did a quick pitter-patter while her palm suddenly felt slick against the glass. Her nerves heightened while she fought a panic that surged through her.

"I think it must be something or you wouldn't have brought it up." The older man made himself comfortable at the table, crossing one booted foot over the other.

"Well, he just isn't your average guy," she began then took a quick gulp of her water. "He says he can do things."

She stopped, giving the older man the once-over. This was nuts. Purely insane. She didn't know Birk at all. She'd been left alone in Merco's house, and how well did she know him?

Birk nodded, not saying anything and letting the silence linger between them. Something crawled through Naomi, an uneasiness followed by a nasty chill.

The creature. The nasty demon was back.

Her hands shook and she put the glass on the counter quickly, wrapping her arms around her waist while she turned her back to Birk.

Birk said something that she didn't hear. She did her best to ignore the crawling terror that worked its way through her body. "You're safe here," he was saying. "Are you okay?"

She nodded vigorously, closing her eye while she batted hair from her face. Sweat had broken out on her forehead. The creature's hands were on her now. That clammy chill of his touch made her skin crawl. She wanted to run, to scream, to yell at it to stay away, leave her alone. Letting out a huge sigh, she ran her fingers through her hair.

"Have you been enjoying being a god's tramp?" The eerie whisper traveled through her like poison, making her gut clench, a knot lodge in her throat making it hard to breathe. "You are my slut, my payback. They will pay dearly and you are my means of revenge."

"What are you talking about?" she whispered. It took all of her energy to take a step forward, reach out and grip the counter.

Again Birk said something behind her. But she couldn't concentrate, couldn't get her thoughts in order. If only Merco were here. He'd left her and the creature had reappeared. She needed Merco.

"Are you okay?" Birk asked again. He reached for her, his touch scorching her skin after the cold sensations that had rippled through her from the nasty creature.

She jumped. The creature laughed. It was a hideous hissing sound that crawled through her veins, making her blood curdle, her muscles clench in rebellion. She wanted him out of her. Gone. Now.

"Maybe you should sit down for a minute." Birk was guiding her backwards, easing her into the chair.

Naomi fought to keep her thoughts straight. The creature, this terrible beast, had left her alone for the past day or so. When Merco was with her there had been no sign of him.

Coward, she thought in her head. *You're scared of him. That must mean he is stronger than you, more powerful. There is no way you will conquer him.*

"Stupid bitch," the demon screamed at her. "It is power that makes me stronger every day. Every time he touches you, I am growing stronger. And he will pass you around. All of his friends will fuck you, too. You know that, don't you? They will lose their strength and I will be invincible. And all because you are a little slut."

His laughter pierced her ears, made her want to puke. She had no idea what he was talking about. His psychobabble made no sense. But something did catch her attention.

Before he had wanted her home—alone. Now he wasn't saying a thing about her leaving Merco's house.

Was this creature using her to get back at Merco?

She needed to think. But there was no way she could figure any of this out because she didn't have all of the answers. She didn't know who Merco was, or what he was. He'd told her that he was immortal, a god, but that was nothing more than mythology. Or was it?

Naomi shook her head, all of this seeming like a wild dream. She had sought out the unknown, grasped what many already viewed as ridiculous. Thena studied witchcraft, and knowledge like that excited Naomi. So what was wrong with going one step further, accepting the fact that powerful beings existed, that the world didn't hover around simple humans such as herself?

"Maybe something a little stronger than water," Birk said, hovering over her. "Merco will be here soon."

Naomi nodded, not paying much attention to the man. Her thoughts spun, fighting to keep the creature at bay while desperately trying to see all of a picture that just wasn't there. If she could just get her heart to quit pounding, her hands to quit shaking. Surely she could figure out the best way to attack this creature, get him out of her head.

"I don't think Merco should be here." She didn't know what this creature was about, but he was telling her things he hadn't mentioned before. And she didn't want Merco hurt.

"Oh, yes. Let Merco come." The creature chuckled, a drawn-out wheezing sound. It vibrated through her, making her feel sick. "He will fuck you. Oh, yes. I will lay with you, feel his cock thrust in and out of your hot cunt. Your muscles will tighten around him, choke him. I will be with you when you ride him, you little slut. You will beg him to fuck you. Beg him to come inside you again. It will be a hot little ride. You know you can't wait."

"You're sick," she told him, disgusted to the point that her tummy revolted, her throat burning with nausea.

"I beg your pardon?" Birk said, turning around from his search of the kitchen cabinets.

"I wasn't talking to you," she told him quickly. There was no way she could explain this to him.

She jumped up, hurrying out of the kitchen, not wanting to make a fool out of herself in front of Merco's friend. It was all she could do to climb the stairs. The nasty creature groped at her, fondling her, his long bony fingers sliding over her hips, squeezing her ass. His clammy touch made her skin crawl. The urge to puke overwhelmed her.

But she had to fight it. She had to keep her wits about her. There had to be a way to overcome this awful being who wouldn't leave her alone.

A thought occurred to her. Merco had told her that Bridget and Braze were like him. She had seen the two of them disappear into thin air.

"Bridget," she whispered, reaching the top of the stairs on her hands and knees.

The carpet rubbed through the long underwear, burning her knees.

"Bridget. Can you hear me?" she called out louder. "God. If you are what Merco says you are, I demand that you show up here. Come to me, right now."

She was nuts. Absolutely insane. Now she was trying to master telepathy when she had never even given it a thought as something that really existed.

"What are you doing?" the creature hissed. "No one can save you. You are a foolish, stupid bitch."

"Bridget," she screamed, burning her throat.

Gentle hands, warm and smooth, brushed the hair away from her face. She looked up, standing and facing her friend.

Bridget didn't look happy at all.

Naomi licked her lips. This was her friend. She had known Bridget for years. They had laughed together, cried together, gotten drunk together. There was nothing to fear with her friend. She swallowed, meeting her stare.

"I need your help," she whispered, wondering if she shouldn't be panicking that she'd just managed to make her appear out of thin air.

Bridget inhaled slowly, letting it out, while she assessed Naomi's appearance.

"What has he done to you?" she asked, taking her friend by the arm.

Naomi didn't realize how unsteady she was until Bridget steadied her.

It dawned on her though that the creature was gone. Her thoughts were clear. She looked down at herself, mentally taking inventory. She didn't feel him touching her. She didn't sense him inside her.

"He's scared of you, too," she mused, and caught Bridget cocking her head at her, staring at her intently. She attempted a weak smile. "Bridget. Merco told me some things. You are here. So I guess he must have been right."

"Who is scared of me?" her friend asked.

Naomi realized everything Merco had said was true. Bridget didn't react to her words that Merco had revealed they were different. Of course she wouldn't. Bridget already knew that. But she did react to someone fearing her. Now to try and explain the impossible.

"Naomi. Something is tormenting you. We sense that. You need to tell me who it is." Bridget ran her hand up Naomi's arm, a comforting gesture.

Something sounded downstairs. Voices. Merco had returned. He exchanged a few words with Birk and then appeared at the bottom of the stairs. His friends were with him. Bridget's grip tightened on her arm.

"What's going on here?" He took the steps two at a time until he was next to her, and then pulling her into his arms. "Bridget?"

A silence fell around them. They were communicating. Naomi sensed it. She looked up at Merco and then into Bridget's face. Bridget had a stern expression. Merco appeared relaxed, his warm body pressing protectively against hers.

She glanced over at Morph and Ace as they climbed the stairs slowly, joining everyone on the landing. They had a mixture of curiosity and concern on their faces. None of them said a word. But for some reason she just knew all of them were having a heated conversation.

There was one way to find out for sure. "Stop it!" she yelled in her thoughts.

Every one of them looked at her, surprised.

Naomi pushed her way out of Merco's arms, brushing past Bridget toward Merco's bedroom and then turned in the wide hallway that overlooked the stairs. She stared at all of them. Bridget looked concerned. Merco was hard to read, his expression blank but a small muscle twitched along his jawbone, her only clue that he suppressed whatever emotions he felt. Ace and Morph glanced at the others, and then back at her. Ace offered her a small reassuring smile.

"All of you are telepathic." Dear God. Of course they were. She just summoned Bridget. They had all heard her yell in her head. She knew they had because their body language changed, and they'd all given her their attention. She rubbed her hands over her face. "This is all too much to handle."

"I know it is," Bridget said soothingly, coming to her with open arms. "Merco shouldn't have done this to you. It won't help what plagues you at all."

Naomi accepted the hug, returning it and relaxing in the comfort of her friend's arms. "It's not Merco. He hasn't done anything wrong. I saw you and Braze disappear the other day. He owed me an explanation."

Naomi pulled back, looking her friend in the face. "And I admit it freaked me out. But with everything going on right now, I think I can handle the knowledge." She attempted a laugh, trying to feel strong, but she quivered, and pulled back again.

"So what's plaguing you has come back," Merco said, taking a step forward.

His earnest expression, the way he watched her, looking so full of concern, a desperate gaze that would do what it took to help her. She wanted to run to him, tell him everything the nasty creature had said. At the same time she was embarrassed, remembering what Bridget had said, knowing Merco had a reputation for being a bit adventurous sexually. She wished she knew what past encounters he'd experienced, but had a feeling the knowledge would make her jealous as hell.

"Yes. I think he's scared of you," she said.

"I'm sure he is." Merco's tone grew dark, sending chills through Naomi. He suddenly looked like a man to be scared of. "The bastard won't show himself around me."

"Merco says you saw a figurine that resembled the creature in your head," Bridget prodded.

"Yes. It was him. It didn't look like him. It was him." Naomi wrapped her arms around her waist, suddenly cold.

Bridget rubbed her chin, looking worried. "According to Merco the figurine was a replica of the demon leader, the ruler of all hells."

Naomi felt the blood drain from her face, fear gripping her, and she fought to steady her breathing. "The devil?" she whispered, unable to stop the terror that wrapped around her.

She was being haunted by the devil?

Bridget made a face. "That is a human word."

"I am human," Naomi argued, needing to make sense out of all of this. Her head was spinning. "And I'm not crazy. That figurine was the creature in my head."

"That just doesn't make sense." Bridget appeared lost in thought, as if trying to remember something. "I told him to go away..."

She suddenly snapped her fingers, her mouth opening as if suddenly she had figured something out. "Braze," she yelled.

Naomi sensed someone behind her. Braze's soft aftershave scent greeted her before she turned around. She jumped, startled, when Bridget's boyfriend smiled at her and then looked over her shoulder at the others.

"Holy shit," she cried out, and then grabbed her heart, which had begun pounding a mile a minute. "I'm not sure I can get accustomed to this."

"You shouldn't have done that to her," Merco argued, pushing past Bridget to get to Naomi.

"You're the one who told her about us," Braze pointed out.

Once again Merco wrapped her into his arms. It felt damn good there.

She leaned against him. "It's okay. If this is who you are, I guess I better get accustomed to it."

Another silence fell around them and she watched Bridget move to Braze, while Merco's friends crossed their arms as if listening intently.

"Cut that out," she said, looking up at Merco. "All of you are talking to each other. I know you are. It's not fair to leave me out of the conversation."

"You're right, and I think the mistake is mine," Bridget said quietly. "There is something I am going to tell you. And I can only hope you won't hate me once you know."

Chapter Sixteen

Naomi accepted the sweet iced tea that Birk offered her as she sat on the terrace. She'd gone outside for some fresh air with Bridget while Merco, Braze and the others had shut themselves in a room for a private argument. She ached to know what they were talking about.

The faint sound of the doorbell ringing inside grabbed her attention, and she wondered who in the hell else could possibly be here.

"Marlita." Bridget stood from where she'd been lounging on the other side of the terrace. Her breath clouded in front of her in the brisk air when she spoke. "What are you doing here?"

An older woman took a step or two outside and then zipped up her jacket. Naomi recognized her as the shopkeeper of the store where she'd seen the figurine of the creature who plagued her. A nasty chill rippled through her. Why would the woman be here?

"The coven of Hedel has word that a human has learned of you," she began, and then stopped when she noticed Naomi, who remained sitting, legs pulled up to her chest on the large white whicker chair.

"It's okay, Marlita." She gestured to Naomi. "This is my very dear friend, Naomi. You met her with Merco, I believe."

This was insane. The shopkeeper was part of them, too. Her world was caving in around her. Nothing was as she'd thought it was. And she wasn't sure she could take learning much more.

The older woman was small, with a motherly look about her. Long gray hair was wrapped in a tight braid wound into a bun at the top of the back of her head. Her skin was smooth, but when she offered a smile, wrinkles spread over her cheeks. Watery blue eyes showed her concern. Naomi guessed that the woman already knew the situation.

"What is the coven of Hedel?" she asked, glancing from Bridget to Marlita.

The men chose that moment to appear in the doorway, dwarfing Marlita as they gathered around her.

"All of us are a part of that coven," Merco answered her question, looking too damned good in the faded blue jeans he'd donned, paired with a forest green wool sweater. His dark complexion added appeal to the attire, making him stand out among the other men.

Naomi felt her insides grow warm, in spite of the brisk outdoors. She took a sip of her tea, her mouth suddenly too dry. It was impossible to take her eyes off of that magnificent body.

"How much are you going to tell her?" Birk asked, stepping around the men carrying a platter of sandwiches.

"She will know everything." Merco spoke with such conviction the group fell silent.

And for once, Naomi didn't think they were communicating with each other. They appeared to all be dumbfounded.

"Bridget," Merco said, turning his attention toward her. "You will tell Naomi what you did."

Bridget let out a sigh, nodding, but looking down, her long brown hair flowing around her face, masking her expression. Braze moved to stand behind her, rubbing her arms as if she needed support for some task.

"Over a year ago, I discovered that the leader of all of the demons was responsible for stealing my memory. I hadn't known who I truly was for quite a long time. When you met me, I thought I was just like you." Bridget didn't look up until now. Her soft green eyes were watery, and she smiled weakly at Naomi. Braze hugged her from behind, and Bridget sighed, continuing. "When I found out the demon leader had done this terrible thing, he retaliated. He stole you and took you into the hells."

"What?" Naomi couldn't make sense out of any of this. Her stomach twisted in knots. Suddenly the cold air made it real hard to breathe. She was sure she had been asked to accept the impossible already. But this was pushing it over the edge. "Bridget. This demon leader, as you call him, he only started haunting me a few months ago."

"Listen to me." Bridget stepped forward, but Merco moved in front of her, walking over to Naomi.

"I know all of this is hard for you to believe. But knowing the truth is the only way you will be rid of him." He'd never spoken with so much compassion.

Naomi couldn't stop her heart from pounding in her chest. She ached to reach out to Merco, seek the comfort she knew she would find in his arms. None of this made any sense. These people—her friends—were something more than human. Just when she thought she might not be crazy, and possibly could accept the unacceptable, they were throwing her a loop she just wasn't sure she could jump through.

"What do you mean he took me into the hells?" She hated how weak her voice sounded.

Merco stood next to her, tall and powerful. Just his presence assured her she was safe. But this new information, on top of seeing her friends disappear and appear in front of her eyes, in spite of worrying how Merco accomplished his unexplainable actions, was simply too much. She felt like a fool, a weak and helpless nitwit, with this man, this perfect person looking down on her. Nothing on the cover of any magazine came close to his perfection, his dominating persona. And it made no sense that he was so interested in her. It made even less sense that any of this could possibly be true.

"Naomi. He took possession of your body, of your soul, and took you with him." Bridget laughed, although it was a hollow, unhappy sound. "Just how you saw us disappear. That day over a year ago, I watched you disappear."

Naomi shook her head. She couldn't accept any of this. "I don't remember any of that, Bridget. You aren't making sense."

"I know you don't." Bridget wiped a tear that started to fall down her cheek. "And I swear I thought I was doing what was best for you when I wiped it all from your memory."

"You did what?" Not even movies came across sounding this bizarre. Naomi shook her head, doing her best to try and absorb all of this but simply wanting to deny it all. That would be so much easier. But something inside her told her that Bridget spoke the truth. "What did you wipe from my memory? How?"

"Damn it. No one should have to witness the tortures of hell. It was an awful experience. But on that day, I destroyed the demon leader, too. Or I thought I did." Bridget reached her hand out to Naomi, but when Braze wrapped his arms around her, she collapsed back into him, looking crushed. "I am so sorry, Naomi. It wasn't until you told us what the creature looks like inside you that I realized what I had done."

"What you had done?" Naomi couldn't make sense out of this. She shook her head, her heart so heavy in her chest the pain was unbearable. She was scared to ask, her insides so thick with panic that she could hardly breathe. But she had to know. She had to ask the right question that would make all of this clear. "What did you do?"

"I cast the demon leader away. I wanted to punish him for taking my life, for stealing my memory. I didn't even know who Braze was, and I'd loved him for centuries, then disappeared on him, leaving him searching forever trying to find me. Braze helped restore my memories, helped me see who I was. But when I realized the demon leader was responsible I told him to go away. I wanted him gone, out of my sight. And that is what happened."

Naomi just stared at her friend. She couldn't think of anything to say. What she had just heard was worse than any morbid fairy tale. For years she had considered herself more open-minded than most, more willing to accept what most refused to even look at. But this—this story—was simply too much. Yet somehow, through the twisting knot that grew in her stomach, and through the dull throb that started at her temples, she knew what Bridget said was true.

"You made him disappear so that you couldn't see him." Naomi suddenly felt like everything around her was spinning. She white-knuckled the handles of the chair she sat in, her legs cramping from how tight she'd been holding them together while listening.

"That is what we've feared has happened," Merco said, squatting down so that he stared her in the eye. His green eyes penetrated through her, devouring her with the intensity of his stare. He covered her hand with his, the heat from his touch rushing through her like smoldering lava. "Bridget banished him so that she couldn't see him, so that he was gone from her sight, from her life. Her spell on him made it so that none of us could see him. But it didn't make him quit existing."

Her breath came in gasps. Suddenly she couldn't make her mouth work to speak. She pulled her attention away from his stare, needing to think. Looking down at his larger hand covering hers, she tried to steady her breathing.

"And you think he lodged himself in me somehow?" she managed to ask.

"You told us he was the figurine in Marlita's shop," Merco said quietly. "We can get him out of you. But Naomi, I need your trust."

Naomi looked up at him and noticed immediately that his green eyes had darkened. Something had stirred inside him, something raw, unleashed. Her heart fluttered, the warmth of his touch making her feel so hot all of a sudden, she didn't want to think about any nasty creature.

"I don't see that I have much of a choice," she whispered, knowing more than anything she wanted this demon creature, this leader of all the hells, to be gone.

"Yes. You do." Bridget shoved her hair over her shoulder, startling Naomi with the quickness of her words. "Naomi. You don't have to do anything that you don't want to do. I can get that demon out of you. I promise. Let me try."

"You might be able to," Merco acknowledged, turning his attention to Bridget briefly. But he then looked back at Naomi, his fingers starting a slow caress over her skin. "Or you can turn your trust over to me, Naomi. I will take care of you, if you will allow it."

There was something more to what he was saying. Naomi didn't need powers to tell that Bridget spoke out because she was concerned, worried for her friend's sake. And it was worry over more than just the demon inside her.

"I can tell you that I trust you," she said. "But how can I prove it? Words mean nothing. You say you will take care of me." She pulled her hand out from under his, waving to the beautiful setting around them. "But a plush surrounding, not needing to work, none of that means anything. You can't buy me, Merco. What are you offering in exchange for my trust?"

And was trust all that he wanted? She looked into that handsome face, his expression so intent and controlled. Was he capable of love? A man with his incredible looks, capable of having anything he wanted, and more than likely anyone, would he be satisfied with someone as simple as her?

If he read her thoughts, he gave no indication. He stared at her for a long moment, the others surrounding them silent, allowing the two of them that moment. She suddenly worried that she had asked too much. Merco was a being far too incredible for her to understand. More than likely he'd never worked, did whatever he wanted, had any woman that he wanted. For her to ask him to offer her anything in exchange for her trust was too much.

She sighed, looking down, the chill of the day suddenly wrapping around her.

"Come with me," Bridget said suddenly. "I think I can work my way into where that demon is hiding."

Naomi looked up at Bridget's extended hand. An emptiness swarmed through her when Merco said nothing. He stood slowly, a pillar of strength next to her, but completely unreadable. Damn it to hell. She had asked him to voice some kind of commitment to her, and he wouldn't speak. It wasn't fair that they could read each other's thoughts, but she couldn't figure out for the life of her what was going on in Merco's head.

She glanced at Ace and Morph, who stood silently watching her. Bridget had told her that Merco had unusual sexual habits. The demon had sworn that Merco would share her. Her heart suddenly raced at what trusting Merco might mean. But he wouldn't hurt her. He wouldn't do anything to her that she wouldn't want. No matter that she couldn't read him. She knew that. In her heart, she knew he cared for her, even if possibly she cared for him a bit more.

"No." She met Bridget's gaze, but then looked up at Merco to see that he was watching her with an expression chiseled in stone. His gaze burned with a fire that set her insides to flame, though. She couldn't look away. "I will stay with Merco. I trust him to take care of me."

Chapter Seventeen

Bridget was screaming at him. Merco ignored her, knowing her warnings were moot. She thought he would take advantage of Naomi, use her the way he had the many women he'd created in the past.

That wasn't going to happen.

He turned to Morph. "Do you sense the demon inside her?" he asked with his thoughts, not wanting to alarm Naomi at this point, or alert the demon leader if he were somehow hidden where Merco couldn't find him.

"I need to get inside her, my friend," Morph answered.

Braze had guided Bridget from the terrace, preparing to depart with her. They would disappear out of Naomi's sight. She had been through enough just now, enlightening her as to who possessed her and how he had arrived there.

Naomi sat curled into that chair, her baggy shirt and long underwear unable to hide how beautiful she was. And how vulnerable. Her red hair fell like a shroud over her shoulders, sweeping around her full breasts. Blue eyes looked up at him, her long lashes fluttering down and then up again.

Something tightened inside him, emotions swirling and rising while he gazed down at her. She trusted him. And he'd be damned if he would let her down.

"I think you've had enough for now," he told her, an ache growing in him while he stared down at her.

He wanted to take her away, disappear from all of this and have her to himself.

But he wouldn't be alone with her. As long as the demon leader lurked within her, using her, abusing her, she would never be completely his.

Naomi stood, placing her small hand on his chest. He fought the fury rising in him at the thought that something as despicable and disgusting as the demon leader degraded her. For her he would remain calm, smile reassuringly, assure her that with him all would be okay.

Warmth traveled through him when she smiled back. Something he couldn't identify. Something he'd never felt before crept through him, powerful yet simple. And although he had never felt it before, Merco accepted that he loved her. She would be his, and he would take care of her.

After his watcher and Bridget's watcher left, Merco guided Naomi into his living room where Ace and Morph lounged, the two of them in a quiet conversation about the concerns of the coven. The watchers would report to the coven. They had no choice. They would be interrogated repeatedly, allowing all to know what had occurred here so far, and speculate on what was about to occur. The lot of them could be damned.

"We will worry about that later," he told them, knowing the coven probably already disapproved of his interactions with a human. Like he ever cared whether they approved of his actions in the past. Wanting Naomi was surely not half as bad as some of the things he'd done in the past.

"What is the problem?" Naomi ran her fingers through her long hair, parting it into thirds before she slowly began weaving it into a long braid.

"Many of us feel that interacting with humans isn't wise," Ace told her.

Merco glared at his friend, ordering him silently to be nice, but Ace waved him off, focusing on Naomi. Merco knew both of his friends were attracted to her. Hell. Who wouldn't be? Either of them would be a hypocrite for condemning him for wanting her.

Protective instincts surged through him when he sat down on the couch and pulled her down next to him.

"But you two are here," she was saying, her tone as relaxed as her body when she relaxed next to him. "And you are willing to help me."

"Yes," Ace said.

Morph nodded as well.

"What do I have to do?" She looked up at Merco.

Her warmth traveled through him, arousing him, making him hard with need.

"Morph will enter your dreams. Ace will heal the damage the demon has done. And I will be your strength through all of this, offering speed to your recovery." It was the simplest answer he could give her.

She nodded, but her blue eyes clouded, showing her confusion. "All of you are strong in different areas," she said, surprisingly understanding more than maybe even she realized.

"We all have certain gifts, yes." He pulled her closer. "Just as you do."

She smiled, and a soft flush spread over her cheeks. Her gaze darted to his friends, and then down to her hands. She was preoccupied with an anticipation of what the three of them might do to her. And it excited her. He knew she was nervous, but curious, too. She wondered what it would be like to have all three of them fuck her. It was so much more than that, but that was the level she focused on.

The three of them entering her would make her stronger, bring out the natural gifts he believed she possessed. Each of them would leave a bit of their powers with her, making Naomi more in tune with her surroundings, and the ability to control her environment. She would never be a goddess, never an immortal. But Naomi had gifts. She sensed things many humans ignored. The three of them fucking her would strengthen those gifts.

Merco knew if she trusted him, truly trusted him, he would offer her to Ace and Morph. And although she'd voiced her trust and agreed to stay with him, he sensed her hesitation, the worry that ran through her. She needed time.

But the demon leader wouldn't allow her that much time. If he stayed inside Naomi too much longer, he might consume her. Merco wouldn't lose this beautiful creature to such raw evil.

"And what gifts do I have?" she asked, looking up at him.

A sensual hue floated in her blue orbs, making his insides soar, his needs heighten. He would have to fuck her soon. If anything, to show her that he cared, that with him she would always find solace, that nothing like this would ever happen to her again.

"You are strong and you aren't scared." He didn't hesitate. There were so many other things that came to mind, surprising him. He could sing her praises all night long.

Without thought, he ran his hand down her arm. She curved into him, looking into his eyes with questions, and a passion that stole his breath.

"I'm terrified." A shiver rushed over her.

He ran his finger down her cheek, tracing a line over her soft flesh, so warm and smooth. If there was any way he could swallow her terror, give her the gift of confidence, he would do it without hesitating.

So many times in the past he'd created his woman of choice for an evening, delicately creating her personality to suit his mood. That wasn't an option with Naomi. She came to him, flesh and blood, her intricate nature so defined and alive. To alter her would be a heinous crime. He wanted her just as she was, hesitating yet strong, beautiful and intelligent, her free will such an attraction he wondered why he'd wasted centuries ignoring the real thing.

"Are you sure you can make the demon go away?" she asked, glancing at his friends. "How will you do it if you can't even see him?"

"We will enter you, see what you see," Ace told her.

"But right now I don't see him." She shook her head, nestling further into Merco. She worked to make sense of it all. "Whenever I am with Merco, he isn't around."

She licked her lips. His cock lengthened in his pants, surging to life over the slight movement of her mouth. His mind boiled with frustration and anger knowing that even though the despicable demon leader hid, he remained lodged in her. Nothing had ever overtaken Merco, nothing. The demon leader wouldn't be the first.

"Do you think he is with you now?" Morph asked.

Merco sensed that he already had started his own searching, his concentration level peaking even though he appeared relaxed sitting across from them in one of his overstuffed chairs.

Naomi hesitated. "I'm not sure. I think he is. For some reason he feels safer inside me." She cringed. "And I don't know how to explain it. But it just makes me feel so dirty, used."

"None of this is your fault," Merco told her, tipping her chin back so she would look at him. "You must know that."

"I do. I don't think it's anyone's fault." She searched his face, her soft blue eyes wide, showing all of her fears, and her faith in him. "You'll be able to make him go away, won't you?"

He would do more than simply cast the demon leader out of her. "Yes," he said, the fire burning in him mounting as he thought of what he would do to that bastard once he had him out of Naomi.

Merco intentionally made the rest of the afternoon a casual affair. Naomi needed to get accustomed to his friends, feel relaxed around them. By nightfall they had steaks going on the grill out back. He allowed her to witness small feats of their powers. She clapped her hands and laughed when Ace pointed a finger at the grill and created a perfect fire for the meat to cook on. Of course, Ace, being the show-off that he was, then allowed potatoes in foil to appear one at a time and then juggled them for her before easily placing them among the hot coals.

"Your friend is such a ham." She had wrapped her arms around Merco's waist, looking more alive and content than he'd seen her in days. "This is the perfect ending to this day."

"The day isn't over yet." He loved watching her blue eyes darken with passion at his suggestive comment.

She stretched up against him, catlike, pressing her large breasts against his chest. "What creative activity could you possibly have lined up next?"

Merco grinned, enjoying how she felt next to him. A perfect fit. The fire made her red hair glow, bringing out highlights in it as it tumbled past her shoulders in two thick braids, tickling his arm as the thick pleated hair brushed over him.

"Exactly what you need, my dear," he told her.

She tasted of the wine she'd been sipping when he kissed her. Her lips were full and moist, so warm in spite of the cold evening. And when she stretched further along him, wrapping her arms around his neck and drawing herself nearer to deepen the kiss, the protective instincts he had felt earlier swarmed to life inside him, hardening him to stone.

"Mine," he whispered into her mouth.

"Yours?" she asked, her lids low over her eyes, her face aglow in the dim light.

"Oh, yes." And he meant it. With every fiber of his being he knew there was no way he would let her get away from him.

"Mmm." She stretched against him, reaching to kiss him again.

What he wouldn't do to make a meal out of her. Twisting her hair through his fingers, the loose braid holding the strands tight, he willed it to be loose, the way he liked it. She chuckled into his mouth when her hair suddenly flowed free, his to run his hands through as he pleased.

"You two aren't going to be hungry for supper," Ace teased, walking past them with a large plate full of steaks.

He had donned a chef's apron, enjoying the role of cook, and grinned when Merco straightened for fresh air and glared at him over Naomi's head.

She turned in his arms, watching Ace as he carried the food into the dining room. It would do her good to have a large meal. Naomi would need her strength for the evening that would follow.

"You've given me one of the best days I've had in quite a while," she said later, after they had left Ace and Morph lounging in the living room.

"I wanted you relaxed, and ready for the evening." He led the way into his bedroom and then turned around. "There is only one way for you to be relaxed enough, and strong enough, to rid you of the demon."

Moonlight filtered through the window, casting shadows over both of them. But even in the darkness, her blue eyes glowed. There was a flush on her cheeks, and her mouth had formed a perfect pouting expression. She pondered his words for only a second.

"And what is that?" she asked, her words coming on a hushed breath.

He stroked her cheek, her warmth scalding his senses. She would enjoy what he had to offer, and that made his blood boil with anticipation. Sharing her with his friends would truly make her his. And he knew this wouldn't be the same as when he'd shared women with his friends in the past. Naomi was his. His friends knew that. Allowing them to enter her would give her strength, help open up the powers he believed already existed inside her.

This wasn't something she'd ever done before, but she would be willing for him. And the pleasure he would show her would surpass anything she'd ever experienced.

"All three of us will fuck you." His cock throbbed at the thought. "There is no other pleasure like it for a woman."

"And you want to share me?" she asked, running her tongue over her lips. She turned her head into his hand, looking up at him with questioning eyes. "Don't you want me for yourself?"

"Oh, yes. I want you." Merco smiled and reached for her. She wanted to be his. His heart had never felt so light, or beat so hard. "I want to give you paradise, spoil you like you've never been spoiled before. Make you truly mine. And giving yourself to us in this way will make you stronger so we can get rid of the demon leader once and for all."

She blinked once. A slow smile formed on her face as she took a long slow breath. "I've never been with three men before. Hell, I've never been with two men before."

"My dear, then you are about to experience the treat of a lifetime." He pulled her to him hard enough that she collapsed into him.

Moving backwards, he collapsed onto the bed with her. Her body was soft where his was hard, making a perfect fit. She stretched catlike over him, crushing her mouth to his, aroused by his sudden action.

His hands were all over her. She made him wild with her sudden lust, her need to return the aggressive act. Her smaller hands ran down his arms, and then pressed, pushing them upward so that they lay on either side of his head.

"You may be some kind of magical sorcerer, but that doesn't mean you always get to be in charge." There was a mischievous gleam in her eyes when she pushed herself up on him.

The shirt she wore was suddenly way too baggy. It blocked his view of her breasts. He didn't attempt to unpin himself from her grasp. Her body pressed against his, the willowy length of her legs intertwining with his.

"Your clothes are in the way." He had no problem with her playing like she was in charge. Her fiery energy had him hard as a rock and he was in no hurry to make her stop.

"Oh, yeah? And what are you going to do about it?" She hardened her grip on his forearms.

He didn't hide his smile. "Holding me down will not stop me from having you."

She raised an eyebrow, pinching his skin with her fingers. Naomi was up to the challenge of taking him on. His powers didn't sway her, and he loved that he didn't intimidate her.

"What are you going to do? Use your sorcery on me?"

"I'm not a sorcerer."

She lowered her head, running her tongue over his collarbone. If she kept that up his toes would curl up to his knees.

"Then what are you?" Her breath tickled his neck.

Fire rushed through him, his body temperature soaring out of control.

It was all he could do to concentrate. Her lips burned his skin with soft kisses while she traced a hot path down the edge of his shirt.

But she deserved an honest answer. "On Earth, I was known as a god."

She purred, the vibration sending chills rushing through him.

"You are most definitely a god."

Chapter Eighteen

Passion ripped through Naomi, tearing at her senses. She was drunk on Merco. Never before had she felt more alive, more in control, more willing to please a man, and be pleased.

He had told her that he cherished her more than he'd ever cherished anyone before. She wouldn't try to understand what type of life he must have had before meeting her. There wasn't time to focus on that right now. All that mattered was his confession of feelings, of needing her, of wanting her.

And she wanted him. Damn. The need surged through her with enough electricity to light up all of Kansas City. She was alive. On fire. And nothing would hold her back.

She scraped her teeth over his flesh, running her tongue along the edge of his shirt, tickling his skin. A growl erupted from him. Something deep inside him had stirred. She felt it rumble through his body, his muscles hardening underneath her. His arms flexed, and she tightened her grip, holding him in place with all of her strength.

"You can handle it," she murmured, loving the power she felt.

"Oh, yes. I can." He leapt forward, straightening to a sitting position and overpowering her with a smooth swoop.

"Oh!" Before she could stop him he had come down on top of her, twisting around so that he was settled over her.

Her breath caught in her throat. For a moment she couldn't think. Her heart raced so hard all she could do was look up at him in the dimness, the cocky expression on his face exhilarating.

"I don't need powers where you are concerned." His tone had turned dark, something primal emerging from him. "But since you are fascinated by them, I will show you a little trick."

She held her breath, not daring to move. Her body was on fire, a throbbing between her legs so distracting she couldn't think.

He adjusted himself slightly, the bulk of his weight not on her, but still managing to hold her in place. Reaching with one hand, he gripped her shirt, twisting the front of it in his fist. In the next instant he lifted it off of her as if it had simply rested over her and not on her.

"That's not fair." A chill in the room rushed over her suddenly exposed skin. Her nipples hardened instantly, a tingling ache in her breasts urging her to arch into him. "I can't do that to you."

"You can't?" He cocked an eyebrow, his expression turning mischievous. "You have little faith in yourself."

She didn't take her gaze from his as she reached up, managing to free one hand from underneath him, and took a hold of his shirt. It slipped off of his body as easily as hers had.

"Holy shit." She had the sudden urge to start giggling.

And then she realized what he had done. He had lightened the moment, making her giddy. His friends would fuck her tonight. She had no idea how it would play out, or when he'd discussed it with him. The sudden thought of it tied her tummy in knots. Having Merco was all that she needed. But what he offered her, three men pleasuring her at once. What an experience! And he wanted this. He told her that he cherished her and that he wanted to share her. Excitement and fear swarmed through her at the same time.

Merco must have sensed her sudden shift in thoughts. He lowered his head, kissing her gently. The softness of his lips did magic on her. His body pressed against hers, flesh against flesh, his chest hairs tickling her senses. Fire rushed through her, building, growing as a pressure ballooned inside her.

Naomi squirmed underneath him, the urge to come drumming through her. She was drowning, absolutely sinking into an abyss of need and lust. Passion dripped through him as he intensified the kiss.

It took a minute for her to realize her long underwear was gone, and so were his jeans. More magic. The work of a god. But she didn't care. Nothing mattered at this point. She ran her legs along his, his coarse body hair rough against her skin. He was so solid, so hard—very hard. The length of his cock throbbed between them, demanding attention, refusing to be ignored.

"Your mouth is on fire, baby," he whispered, a rough guttural sound. "I need my cock in there. Let me fuck your mouth."

She squirmed underneath him before she had a thought. No longer did she care about dominating him. Nothing mattered anymore other than having him, tasting him, feeling the length of his cock.

Merco moved so that she could sit, straighten and then go to her knees. Bending over on the bed she ran her tongue over his cock head, tasting his salty precum. Her mouth filled with his lust, quickening deep inside her, the fire in her cunt soaring to boiling point.

"Oh, fuck, yeah, baby. You are incredible. Do you know that?"

His words gave her power. It surged through her like a lightning bolt, knowing what she did made him groan with such pleasure. Her mouth stretched over him. She sucked in his hardness, moving her ass as the ache inside her surged out of control.

Resting on her hands and knees, her pussy ached. Her breasts hung full and swollen, craving his touch.

Merco ran his hands over her shoulders, down her back, and then to her head, holding her while she took him in, sucking and licking. Everywhere he touched her sent her nerve endings ablaze. She wouldn't be able to take much more before she exploded.

"That's it, baby. Damn. You could do that all night."

More than anything she wished she could twist her head up, give him this pleasure and be able to see him. He held her head in position, though, his fingers tangling through her hair while it flowed around her, providing a blanket of privacy while she enjoyed the act.

His cock swelled inside her, his fingers tightening their grip as he plunged inside her mouth, pushing his cock down her throat. She gagged and he released, sliding out of her with a fluid movement that she ached to have in her cunt.

"Can you handle three of these, baby?" His words brought her pause.

Slowly removing him from her mouth, she looked up into his face through blurred vision. His expression was tight, contorted with emotions from the pleasure she'd offered. Her body throbbed with need, the ache inside her so incredible she would die if he didn't fuck her soon.

"When?" she asked, excitement rippling through her while she wondered if she could actually handle it.

What if she couldn't satisfy all of them? What if she wore out before they were done?

"Right now." His words had her heart leaping to her throat.

But before she could think about it, before she could respond, hands were on her ass, moving her. She found herself being turned over, stretched on the bed, while gentle warm, large hands slid to her hips.

Merco was over her, blocking her view, but someone had helped her lie down flat on the bed and was stretching her legs apart.

"Oh, God." She cried out when a mouth found the sensitive spot between her legs, hot and moist against the fire that surged through her.

Her cry escaped from her lips at the same time a dam broke inside her. She raised herself off of the bed, riding the tidal wave that gushed through her.

"That's it, baby. Let Morph taste that sweet cum of yours," Merco whispered in her face and then caught her next cry with his mouth when he kissed her.

She wrapped her arms around him, holding on tight while Morph performed magic of the most basic form on her pussy. His tongue swirled around her clit and then dove inside her swollen pussy, lapping at her juices while she came.

And then someone else was there. Merco shifted, allowing hands to cover her breasts. Another mouth brushed over her nipple, sucking it in and saturating her breast with a heat that brought her next orgasm on with a fury that she couldn't handle. She would die of pure pleasure.

Hands were all over her, stroking and caressing while all of their mouths enjoyed her, tasting and licking, sucking and nibbling. She would lose herself in a world of pleasure. Nothing she had ever experienced could compare with the pleasure they offered.

And then they were moving her again, readjusting her. Naomi opened her eyes to see Merco kneeling between her legs, his cock jutting forth, a weapon of satisfaction that she needed so bad she couldn't speak. Morph and Ace knelt on either side of her, naked with cocks eager to have their turn.

"Please" was all she could say when Merco grabbed her legs, positioning his cock at the entrance of her cunt.

He dove in, sending stars exploding in front of her face. White light erupted. She let out a gasp, his cock filling her with so much intensity that she felt it clear up to her belly button.

The rich scent of man hit her when Ace brought his cock to her mouth. There was no need to think, nothing to worry about. No longer did it matter if she could pleasure them. All fear was gone. They were there to please her. She reached for his cock, allowing only moments to learn its new shape and size before she sucked it into her mouth.

Morph took her free hand and wrapped her fingers around his thick shaft while she sucked and was fucked. Merco dove into her hard, sliding her against the bed as he impaled her. Ace moved in and out of her mouth, his aggressiveness not matching Merco's but his groans letting her know she was pleasing him.

She stroked Morph's cock, noticing how all of them were different yet on fire, hard and ready to please her.

"I think she can handle all three of us." It was Merco's voice but it sounded far away, like a dream.

They moved her again. Her pussy craved to be fucked more, her cum soaking her clear to her ass.

Merco moved on the bed, lying on his back and pulling her over him.

"Straddle me, baby. I'm going to give to you what few men can offer their lady. Tonight you will know the epitome of pleasure." He smiled up at her, his green eyes aflame with passion, glowing in the darkness, while his dark features made her want to cry from the beauty of him.

He was doing this for her. The ultimate satisfaction would be hers, and it pleased him to do this. She loved him more at that moment than she ever knew possible. Her heart swelled, the ache matching the need in her pussy. She was on fire, and all of them were here just to give her the experience of pure satisfaction.

She spread her legs over his large frame, her inner thighs stretching while streaks of fire rushed through her muscles. Coming down on his cock, pressing her hands into the heat of his chest, she buried his cock deep inside her cunt.

"Oh, hell yeah," she sighed, feeling him fill her, stretch her.

He stroked her inner walls, gliding through her moist heat with a surging fire that plunged deep inside.

Humidity soared through her, soaking her skin while she slowly began riding his cock.

"Come here, baby." Merco pulled her to him, kissing her roughly while hands gripped her ass, stroking and caressing the sensitive tight little hole.

Her rear end was exposed. Electric currents shot through her while fingers carefully prodded her ass, stretching the hole and soaking it with her own cum.

Something cold and wet touched her skin, a lubricant spread over her ass making those magical fingers glide in and out of her tight hole with ease. She jumped from the unexpected sensation, her enflamed skin suddenly cooled by the smooth cream.

"Shit. Oh, shit." The sensations that rippled through her blinded her with pleasure.

Merco's swollen cock slid in and out of her pussy while experienced fingers prepared her ass for double penetration. This was something only read about in books, in those taboo magazine stories about fictional people. She was about to take two men in her. Holding her breath, she waited for the second cock to enter her.

"Breathe, baby." Merco's order came at the same time he impaled her with a hungry thrust.

His cock split her in two, her body shivering while another orgasm tore through her body.

"Yes. Okay. Yes." She couldn't think.

Her body writhed with the feeling of Merco fucking her hard, with an aggression she hadn't known from him before.

Then her legs were stretched more, Morph positioning himself behind her. She looked up, seeing Ace's cock not too far from her face. He knelt to the side of them, stroking his long shaft with his fingers while watching the two cocks prepare to fuck her.

The lubricant mixed with her cum, soaking her ass and pussy as the pressure built on her ass. Morph's cock pressed against the tight opening, hesitating only a moment before slowly sliding inside her. Merco slowed his movement, allowing for the entrance while her insides stretched.

She cried out, the shooting pain lasting only a moment before two cocks impaled her, filling her beyond a point she ever could have imagined.

"Hell, yes." Her voice sounded foreign to her, a woman crying out with pleasure most never got to ever experience.

The two men began moving slowly, developing an unspoken rhythm as they stroked her insides from her ass and her cunt.

Her breathing came in gasps, looking up through moist eyes to see Ace's cock right there, throbbing in front of her. She couldn't move her hands, couldn't adjust herself for fear of falling and throwing the two men who fucked her off balance.

Nothing could compare with the intense pleasure that rippled through her, the pressure surging through her with so much force she would explode. She closed her eyes for a moment, sucking in air through her mouth while she focused on the two men fucking her, filling her with smooth strokes that soothed an ache so savage she could die from it.

Ace's cock pressed against her lips before she realized he had moved.

"Take it, baby." Merco's voice was rough, a harsh whisper coming in gasps while his body hardened underneath her. "Take all three of us."

She opened her mouth to allow Ace to slip inside. Three cocks filled her, gliding in and out of her while her body quivered on the edge of an orgasm too intense for her to handle.

"I'm going to come," Morph grunted from behind her.

He began to move faster, sliding in and out of her lubed ass while he pressed his fingers into her flesh.

Merco matched the movement, the two men fucking her with increased speed. Ace slid his cock back and forth against her lips, making her mouth tingle while she held her mouth in place, allowing him to fuck her with the same speed the others did.

"Grr," Merco growled underneath her, his cock swelling in her pussy right before he exploded.

Morph grunted from behind her, gripping her ass while he aided in pushing the pressure inside her to a breaking point.

She shivered, a shock wave plummeting through her as she came with more ferocity than she had before. Hot cum soaked her ass, filled her pussy, exploding inside her with a white fire that lapped at her with flames of incredible passion.

Ace pulled out of her mouth, his own semen squirting from his cock. She lapped at the salty taste, suddenly overwhelmed with her own orgasm. Fiery rushes exploded from her soul, taking all of her strength.

Naomi collapsed on top of Merco, soaked and tingling from head to toe.

Chapter Nineteen

Naomi rolled over in her bed, momentarily disoriented as she stared at the ceiling of her bedroom.

What the hell was she doing here?

It took a moment to wake up, get her thoughts organized. She had fallen asleep in Merco's arms. She was sure of it. She didn't remember coming home, though.

Taking her covers with her as she rolled over, she stared at her quiet room, everything in order. She was very much alone.

"What the hell?" she whispered, and then cleared her throat.

Muscles throughout her body screamed in retaliation as she moved. She was damp in between her legs, her only proof that she hadn't dreamed the previous night.

"I don't even have a phone number." She was instantly grouchy, climbing out of bed and hitting the cold floor with her bare feet.

But what would a god need with a telephone? Furthermore, what would he need with her?

Her grouchiness grew as she traipsed to the bathroom, starting the water and letting it run until it was hot. She climbed into her shower, simply standing there as the pellets of water rushed over her, soothing her tender body. As confused as she was, she couldn't get herself to believe that Merco had used her last night.

Somehow being with the three of them had given her insight. It would be easy to accept the fact that Merco, with his playboy reputation, had gotten what he wanted and was now done with her. It would make sense. Waking up alone, obviously transferred by some feat of magic while she slept. He hadn't told her he would bring her home, there'd been no mention of it. But try as she would, wanting to fall into her own pity party, she knew there was another reason she had awakened alone in her apartment. Now to figure out what that reason was.

She sulked while lathering her hair and then rinsing. Her mood barely lightened as she toweled off and then dressed in a pair of jeans and a sweatshirt.

"Why did you bring me home?" She looked around her silent apartment, feeling foolish.

But this would be how she would contact Merco, right? Just the thought that he could read her mind no matter where she might be overwhelmed her. That is, if he wanted to know her thoughts.

It dawned on her as she went through the motions of preparing coffee that she hadn't given thought to the demon for almost a day. She had Merco to thank for that. If he had in fact just used her, as Bridget warned might happen, then she could at least give thanks that he'd offered her a bit of sanctuary—a respite from her extended nightmare.

"Of course, all he did was use you. What else are you good for?" The slowly hissed words of the demon made her jump.

"Leave me alone," she sighed, already too weary to fight with the nasty creature.

"Leaving you alone is the last thing I'll do." His serpent-like voice sounded clearer, louder than usual. "I've been contemplating your punishment for being such a slut without my consent."

Her tummy turned with fear while an unwelcome shiver tore through her. Something was different about the demon. She stared at the black liquid drip slowly into the glass pot, its rich smell no longer doing anything for her. Licking her lips, she fought for the strength to tell the creature to go away, leave her alone.

"You don't own me. Get out of here before you are the one punished." Her heart beat so hard she could hardly hear herself think. Please don't let the creature know how desperately terrified she was.

Long bony fingers gripped her shoulder, flipping her around with more strength than she would have imagined him having.

Naomi shrieked when she turned to see the demon leader standing in her kitchen, now facing her. He was taller than she, and so gaunt every bone in his body protruded from the paper-thin skin that hung on him. Hideous. Repulsive. He towered over her, his back hunched while bones protruded from his shoulders when he reached for her.

The demon wore no clothing, and a long, too thin cock protruded in a warped angle toward her. His cock head was shriveled, disgusting. Everything about him disgusted her. He was worse than she could imagine death looking. Pale and a gray-green, veins visible under his flesh. She gulped in air that reeked of him, unable to think, to do anything other than stare in complete terror.

"Your little stunt last night has given me strength. No more will you do anything, or anyone, other than who I say." His lips barely covered his teeth. And the stench.

His body reeked so terribly her eyes watered while her stomach turned.

"Merco!" She screamed his name, the first word that came to her lips.

The demon laughed, a despicable raspy sound that made his rib cage expand and his stomach appear more gaunt than before.

"He doesn't care about you. You're a slut. You put out for him and his friends and tonight it will be a different lady. Everyone knows that about him. Don't you read your history books?"

His hands were on her, pinching her skin while he pulled her to him. "And now you will give me everything that you gave them, bitch."

"Fuck you!" Her mouth was almost too dry to speak. She shook beyond control, while her breath came in hard gasps.

Terror had her incapable of fighting him. He was stronger than she imagined, or else she was too stupefied to react. But he pulled her to him, her body slamming against his slimy skin.

"Merco!" she screamed again.

He had to hear her. There was no way he would allow this to happen. He would save her. Dear God. Please.

"Get your fucking hands off of her."

She heard him before she saw him.

Merco appeared behind the demon, grabbing him, pulling him backwards, and throwing him into the living room as if he were no heavier than a bag of potatoes.

"No!!" The hideous scream of the demon leader would wake the dead, and everyone else in the apartment complex.

Suddenly Ace and Morph were in the kitchen, too, crowding her so that she could no longer see anything but the three men, the three gods. Strong, powerful, her saviors.

"Merco," she said on a sigh, the shakes still consuming her body but relief flooding through her faster than her heart raced.

"Let him in your head," Merco said, gesturing to Morph.

She looked over at Merco's friend, who watched her, a calm expression on his face.

"I can protect you better in your thoughts." His mouth hadn't moved. He was already in her mind.

"Yes." She sunk backwards, giving Morph her attention for only a moment before looking back at Merco.

He smiled warmly, a reassuring grin, but there was a fire burning in his eyes. She didn't miss the outrage that made his expression hard, determined. He was out for blood. And she didn't feel one bit sorry for that hideous creature.

"Just relax. You're safe now." Morph spoke to her in her thoughts.

Ace was by her, too, the two gods providing a shield that prevented her from clearly seeing Merco turn and move into the living room after the demon.

"You no longer exist," she heard Merco say, using a tone she prayed she would never hear out of him again.

The demon leader screamed. She could only imagine what story she would have to come up with to satisfy the neighbors when they came pounding at her door. She wouldn't worry about that until it happened. Too much was going on around her.

"From this point forward, your existence has ended. There is no more hiding, no more torturing, you are done." Merco sounded so fierce that she doubted anyone could be more powerful than he was. The man was invincible, and he was hers.

Naomi's heart soared, a peace easing through her allowing her to catch her breath, once again hear the coffee brewing behind her. Ace took her arm, his touch warm and reassuring while his body blocked the view into the living room. Morph also stood next to her, although she knew he was in her mind, ensuring her safety should the demon try to return there.

No more. Her torture session had ended. Merco had saved her, and captured her heart.

When silence fell around the apartment, the calm quiet so typical of her early morning, she felt a peace settle through her that she hadn't known in months.

It was over. Her nightmares would no longer haunt her. When Merco turned, appearing over the shoulder of Ace, she looked up at him, seeing the possessive protector staring down at her.

"It's done," he told her simply.

She hadn't even realized she had moved when she was in his arms, feeling his strength, the warmth of his body and the strength of him wrapping around her.

"I love you," she whispered, unable to help herself, and knowing it was true.

Maybe she'd closed her eyes, maybe he'd used more magic. But when she looked up at him, staring into that beautiful face, it dawned on her that they were all alone.

"Naomi." He said her name like he was praying.

Or at least it sounded that way to her. Never had she felt more cleansed, more at rest, more happy than she did right now.

"Yes?" she asked, her heart suddenly heavy in her chest with anticipation.

She wouldn't be able to bear it if he scolded her for confessing her emotions, or politely told her she was overreacting to his rescue of her. There were no doubts. Merco was different, unlike anyone she ever could imagine. But it was his manner, his calm reassurance, the way he stood tall next to her, willing to battle for her. He was more than a knight in shining armor, more than a god, he was a person, a man. Whether or not he had pushed his way into her life, informed her she wanted him when she thought she hadn't, his cockiness and self-assured attitude simply added to the beauty of him.

Yes. Beyond a shadow of a doubt she loved him. And she was up to the challenge of keeping him in line. And what a challenge that would be. She smiled at the thought.

"You better tell me that you love me, too," she muttered, gliding her hands over his hard body, muscles protruding under his shirt, hard and hot against her fingers.

Merco laughed, wrapping his arms around her, sweeping her off her feet and spinning her around the kitchen.

"Woman. I am head over heels in love with you. And I never thought anyone would make me feel this way." And then he lowered his mouth to hers, holding her tight, her feet hanging above the floor.

She wrapped her arms around his shoulders, holding on tight, while his body pressed hard against hers, bringing her to life.

They fit against each other perfectly, as if it were always meant to be.

Enjoy this excerpt from

Pack Law

Lunewulf

The rich, thick aroma in the air couldn't be mistaken. Everyone here wanted to fuck.

In the living room, Sophie's sister, Trudy, gyrated to the thumping music. Pack members lingered everywhere in the small house, enjoying the party. Some werewolves from a pack south of Prince George had shown up too.

Damp air coming through the window gave her goose-bumps when she passed in front of it, weaving around the people who hovered at the dining room table, munching on the snacks.

Salt, lust, sweat and bitter cigarette smoke permeated the close quarters. Her hair would stink tomorrow. Sophie tucked a blonde strand behind her ear, then leaned against the wall, next to the window, to enjoy the hint of outdoors that trickled in.

Everyone will end up in the corners fucking before the night is over, her cousin Simone had said when she came by to pick up Sophie and her sisters at their grandmother's house.

I want to get fucked tonight. She searched the room to see if *he* had arrived yet—hopefully, it wasn't obvious she didn't care about the party. Ever since she had turned eighteen, *he* had consumed her thoughts. Nik always seemed to be nearby, but she had it on good authority from Simone, that he planned to be at Johann's party.

I'm wherever you are because I am watching you. Nik had stood behind her at the last pack meeting and whispered in her ear. You are mine. Our dens have chosen you for me, and I plan to make my mark very soon.

His wicked promise had kept her on the verge of an orgasm for the past week. Her throbbing clit drove her to distraction. Now, thick cream saturated her panties just thinking about what he'd said. The October breeze seeping through the window did nothing to ease the intense heat of her aching pussy.

"Elsa, wait for me." Sophie's sister left the kitchen, heading for the back door. "I'll go outside with you." Maybe Nik would be outside.

"You aren't having any fun either?" Elsa shoved her long blonde hair over her shoulder. Worry clouded her pretty blue eyes.

Sophie ran her hand over her baby sister's hair. "It's a bit warm in here. But you should relax. You'd have more fun. There are tons of sexy wolves here tonight."

Elsa looked even more troubled, but Sophie couldn't help smiling. Her sister acted like a prude. How could they be from the same den?

When she followed Elsa out the back door, the cold night air slapped her face. A large group circled a bonfire in the corner of the yard. Sophie stepped around her sister to look for Nik.

Her heart pounded faster and blood raced through her veins; the primal urge to change filled her being. The beast in her, the beautiful *lunewulf,* begged to be released. Wood-smoke mixed with the crisp sweetness of the pines growing on the edge of the property. The night air wrapped around her, drawing her nipples to hardened peaks. She loved the cold, the change of autumn to winter. It made her frisky, full of life and the desire to run and play. Rolling in the meadows with a certain tall, well-built *lunewulf* would make the night perfect.

She wandered into the yard toward the bonfire. But the partiers didn't impress her. At the other end, over by the group of parked cars, deep, male baritones grabbed her attention, heightening her lust-torn nerves. Could Nik be with that group?

She glanced back at Elsa. Johann had found her. Good. Her sister would be distracted. Sophie put a strut in her walk, and strolled across the yard. A beer might calm her nerves.

"Looking good, Sophie." Lukas Kade grinned from the other side of the keg, while holding the black tube that pumped beer into a plastic cup. He handed the cup to her, spilling the golden brew over the edges.

"Thanks Lukas." Sophie never knew what to say to the stocky man.

She sipped at the beer and watched over the rim as Lukas approached her. He grabbed her shoulder, his thick fingers squeezing her bones, then leaned in to bury his head in her hair.

"I love your scent. I can almost taste the rich cream from your pussy when I'm near you. We need to get together soon." Thick fingers rubbed against her tummy then moved under her sweater to cup her breast. Calloused roughness brushed her hardened nipple. Electric tingles shot through her, and a nervous sweat broke out over her chilled skin.

Enjoy this excerpt from

Tainted Purity

Fallen Gods

Think hard, Bridget. Remember and come to me.

He whispered the thought into her mind while he reached out and stroked the side of her neck with his finger. So soft, so warm, so vibrant and alive.

Bridget spun around, her look wild while she searched the room. Her hand went to her neck, her fingers touching the spot he had just touched.

"Go away," she whispered, her tone fierce and demanding.

Braze slid backward across the floor, almost losing his footing. Grabbing the side of the wall, he braced himself, disbelief coursing through him while he stared at her. Her fingers lingered at her neck while she looked around, wide-eyed. Her panic reached out to him, her confusion and paranoia.

If he hadn't experienced her powers first hand, he never would have believed it. They had grown ten-fold. Not only were they not dormant, they were incredibly strong.

"Do you remember making this?" Maureen didn't seem aware that Bridget shook with fright.

Braze saw that her expression had paled, the rosy look that had colored her cheeks a moment before gone. As powerful as she was to move him without his consent, a feat none of the elders would have been able to do, Bridget had no clue that she had these powers.

"Maureen. I can't believe you kept that." Bridget managed to compose herself, the fear that had swarmed around her dissipating quickly.

[…]

Maureen held out a zip-lock bag holding an artifact made from straw. "...I remember asking you why you wanted to make a cross like that when you were a child, but you just shrugged at the time and told me that was how it wished to be designed."

Braze moved in closer, looking over Bridget's shoulder at the artifact preserved as well as possible in the plastic bag.

[...]

"I'd just arrived here," Bridget remembered, her thoughts cloudy while she tried to search back to her childhood.

Braze ached to soothe her, ease her memory, take her in his arms and hold her until the unknown pain that blocked her ability to regain what she'd hidden was gone.

"Yes. They found you in the park—half-starved." Maureen watched Bridget's expression, her worry that Bridget wouldn't enjoy the memory as obvious on her face as it was in the air around her.

Braze reached out to Bridget, gently touching her thoughts, searching for what she refused to show. How had she been deserted in a park? Who had her and treated her like this?

Bridget sincerely didn't know who she was. Somehow her memory had been erased, her past lives a mystery to her. Yet her power was intact, burning through her passionately. That part of her reached out to him, carefully, cautiously. Again she showed no fear. She knew he searched her thoughts though, and carefully took a look at him to see who he was and why he did it.

Outwardly though, Bridget frowned, focusing on the older woman. "You gave me a good life," she said finally, giving up internally on finding the lost memories.

Maureen shrugged, reaching for Bridget, her dimpled hand stroking Bridget's arm the way Braze wanted to.

"I'm glad you are happy, sweetheart." She smiled, and then turned toward the box. "And the children will love the gifts that you've brought them."

"Well, I need to keep moving." Bridget shoved him away again.

This time Braze was ready for her, backing out of her thoughts slowly, wanting more than anything to touch her with more than his mind.

"Let me know if you need anything else." Bridget already hurried toward the door.

He'd made her nervous. She believed leaving the room would rid her of whoever it was had nagged at her. *Nagged at her*. That is what she thought he was doing. Once she had gloried in his presence; now he annoyed her. He would absolutely destroy the person who had taken his Bridget from him.

And in the meantime, he wouldn't let her out of his sight. Marching right after her, following her back to her car, he mentally worked to contact a few friends, those he could trust, those who would be able to take the time to search, find out what had happened to her.

He climbed in next to her and watched with patient curiosity while she tried to make her car start.

"Damnit. Start," she yelled, and the machine rattled to life.

She didn't question her powers, her mind refusing to see the obvious, but instead drove away from the orphanage. And she was headed toward her home! He couldn't think of a better place for them to go. Braze doubted he would be able to keep his hands off of her much longer. Just sitting next to her, the full curve of her breasts so nicely accented by the snug-fitting sweater she wore made him ache to be inside her. With every breath, the material stretched, her soft curves enticing, tempting him until his blood boiled. Her tight, flat tummy and long legs made him ache to see her out of those clothes.

Braze itched to reach out and touch her, allow the molecules inside him to form enough so that he could feel the soft warmth of her body against his fingers. Thoughts of making the car break down, of having it turn and take them to some isolated place tempted him. She took too long to reach her home. There wasn't enough power in the universe to keep him from her, and waiting another moment, after being deprived for so many centuries seemed too much to ask.

"You have always been mine," he whispered, although in his thoughts.

He knew she heard him. Those soft green eyes widened, searched the car quickly before returning her attention to the road. He watched her slender fingers wrap around the steering wheel and imagined them gripping his cock as tightly. The fire burning in him intensified, making it hard to control his powers, to keep from forcing himself upon her, force her to remember how once she had screamed his name in pleasure.

His cravings became too much. Just to touch her, to stroke his fingers over her soft, warm skin, to feel her heat flush through him, adding to his own fever, made the drive to her home seem an eternity. She didn't see him, didn't know him, refused to accept that he sat next to her.

But he could let her experience the gentlest of caresses. Her heart would see what her mind refused to. For now, that would be enough.

Braze almost felt the dash come up against him when Bridget slammed on the brakes.

"Get out!" Those green eyes burned with fury when she turned and glared directly at him. "You will leave me alone! Be gone. You will never bother me again."

She yelled the words so loudly her voice cracked. But 'the intensity of her powers succeeded. Braze grabbed a hold of the interior of the car, all of his attention focused on preventing himself from flying out of the car.

"Leave!" She pointed a finger directly at him, the tip of her fingernail almost touching his nose.

"Don't do this, Bridget." He barely got the words out before he was propelled from the car.

About the author:

All my life, I've wondered at how people fall into the routines of life. The paths we travel seemed to be well-trodden by society. We go to school, fall in love, find a line of work (and hope and pray it is one we like), have children and do our best to mold them into good people who will travel the same path. This is the path so commonly referred to as the "real world".

The characters in my books are destined to stray down a different path other than the one society suggests. Each story leads the reader into a world altered slightly from the one they know. For me, this is what good fiction is about, an opportunity to escape from the daily grind and wander down someone else's path.

Lorie O'Clare lives in Kansas with her three sons.

Lorie welcomes mail from readers. You can write to her c/o Ellora's Cave Publishing at 1056 Home Avenue, Akron OH 44310-3502.

The Ellora's Cave Library

Stay up to date with Ellora's Cave Titles in Print with our Quarterly Catalog.

Why an electronic book?

We live in the Information Age—an exciting time in the history of human civilization in which technology rules supreme and continues to progress in leaps and bounds every minute of every hour of every day. For a multitude of reasons, more and more avid literary fans are opting to purchase e-books instead of paperbacks. The question to those not yet initiated to the world of electronic reading is simply: *why?*

1. *Price.* An electronic title at Ellora's Cave Publishing and Cerridwen Press runs anywhere from 40-75% less than the cover price of the exact same title in paperback format. Why? Cold mathematics. It is less expensive to publish an e-book than it is to publish a paperback, so the savings are passed along to the consumer.
2. *Space.* Running out of room to house your paperback books? That is one worry you will never have with electronic novels. For a low one-time cost, you can purchase a handheld computer designed specifically for e-reading purposes. Many e-readers are larger than the average handheld, giving you plenty of screen room. Better yet, hundreds of titles can be stored within your new library—a single microchip. (Please note that Ellora's Cave and Cerridwen Press does not endorse any specific brands. You can check our website at www.ellorascave.com or

www.cerridwenpress.com for customer recommendations we make available to new consumers.)

3. *Mobility.* Because your new library now consists of only a microchip, your entire cache of books can be taken with you wherever you go.
4. *Personal preferences are accounted for.* Are the words you are currently reading too small? Too large? Too...**ANNOYING**? Paperback books cannot be modified according to personal preferences, but e-books can.
5. *Instant gratification.* Is it the middle of the night and all the bookstores are closed? Are you tired of waiting days—sometimes weeks—for online and offline bookstores to ship the novels you bought? Ellora's Cave Publishing sells instantaneous downloads 24 hours a day, 7 days a week, 365 days a year. Our e-book delivery system is 100% automated, meaning your order is filled as soon as you pay for it.

Those are a few of the top reasons why electronic novels are displacing paperbacks for many an avid reader. As always, Ellora's Cave and Cerridwen Press welcomes your questions and comments. We invite you to email us at service@ellorascave.com, service@cerridwenpress.com or write to us directly at: 1056 Home Ave. Akron OH 44310-3502.

ELLORA'S CAVE
ROMANTICA PUBLISHING

Printed in the United States
32064LVS00003B/67-969